"You do reali[...] up, don't you?

Amanda gasped. *She wouldn't!*

But this was Irene they were talking about. She would.

"She knows I'm not looking to date again. And even if I was..." She waved her hand toward Nate, then stopped herself before finishing her thought. She doubted he wanted to hear that he was too old for her. Obviously, she liked older men, but if she ever dipped her toes back into the dating pool, she'd stick with guys closer to her own age.

"Hate to break it to you," Nate said, his dimple winking at her as he pulled onto the road, "but my dad all but admitted their matchmaking plans to me. I thought I talked him down by telling him I'm moving to Boston in the fall, but apparently not."

"Oh, man." Amanda groaned. "I'm sorry she dragged your dad into her scheming. They're going to be *so* disappointed."

He chuckled. "It'll serve them right, though."

"It sure will." She relaxed into her seat. Thank goodness they were on the same page about not dating. Otherwise, this whole maid of honor/best man thing could get awkward fast...

Meghann Whistler grew up in Canada but spent her summers on the beaches of Cape Cod. When she's not reading, writing or jamming out to Christian rock music, you can find her enjoying a relaxing evening with her rocket scientist husband (seriously—he's a real live rocket scientist!) or playing with her three kids. She loves to hear from her readers, who can reach her at meghannwhistler.com.

Books by Meghann Whistler

Love Inspired

Falling for the Innkeeper
The Baby's Christmas Blessing
Their Unlikely Protector
The Pastor's Hope

Visit the Author Profile page at LoveInspired.com.

THE PASTOR'S HOPE

MEGHANN WHISTLER

LOVE INSPIRED
INSPIRATIONAL ROMANCE

LOVE INSPIRED®
INSPIRATIONAL ROMANCE

Recycling programs for this product may not exist in your area.

ISBN-13: 978-1-335-93716-2

The Pastor's Hope

Copyright © 2025 by Meghann Whistler

Love Inspired
22 Adelaide St. West, 41st Floor
Toronto, Ontario M5H 4E3, Canada
www.LoveInspired.com

Printed in U.S.A.

When thou passest through the waters,
I will be with thee; and through the rivers,
they shall not overflow thee: when thou
walkest through the fire, thou shalt not be burned;
neither shall the flame kindle upon thee.
—*Isaiah* 43:2

For my children, who are an endless source of entertainment and inspiration. I love you!

Chapter One

Pastor Nate Anderson steeled himself as he looked at his dad across the kitchen table. He wasn't sure why he was nervous—he was a grown man, almost forty years old. He didn't need his father's permission to leave Wychmere Bay, Massachusetts.

Still, he'd like his dad to be happy for him. This was a dream long deferred.

Nate and his father had just finished clearing the dishes and settled back down for a cup of after-dinner decaf. It had been their nightly routine since his son, Hayden, had been a baby—although now that his father and Irene Perkins were engaged, his dad wasn't around at mealtime nearly as often.

Nate touched his back pocket, where he'd stashed the email he'd printed out from Harvard Divinity School, and took a deep breath. Hayden was out walking the dog, giving Nate the privacy he needed to broach the subject with his dad. *Here goes nothing.*

Before he could say anything, though, his father put down his coffee cup and stroked his salt-and-pepper mustache. "Irene and I set a new date for the wedding."

"You did? That's great!" Nate said, glad for the reprieve. "When is it? I'll add it to my calendar right now."

His dad had been a widower almost as long as Nate. But

from the moment Irene Perkins, the owner of the local candy shop, had agreed to go on a date with him, his father had been full steam ahead. He'd proposed after just three months of dating, although COVID had delayed their wedding plans quite a bit.

"July first," his father said proudly.

"Really? That's soon."

His father grinned and waggled his eyebrows. "We're not getting any younger."

Wasn't that the truth? Nate ran a hand over his own dark hair, which was now sprinkled with gray. "I'm happy for you, Dad."

"You'll officiate, won't you? And we want you and Hayden to be co–best men."

"Oh, wow, of course," Nate said, honored. He and his dad had always been close, but they'd gotten much closer over the last twelve years as they'd raised Hayden together. *Two men and a baby*, his dad used to joke, until Hayden got old enough to take umbrage.

"I not a baby, Gwampa! I a big boy!" his son would say, shaking his little fist.

Then Grandpa Bill would lift him up and do an airplane with him, making Hayden squeal with laughter.

Nate sighed. He missed those days.

Not that he didn't enjoy the time he spent with Hayden now. His son was kind and curious, with a huge appetite for books, chess tournaments and cooking.

And getting to dress up in a tuxedo for his grandfather's wedding? That would be right up Hayden's alley.

"He'll love that."

His father's face lit up. "We thought he would. You'll like the maid of honor, too. Sweet gal, Irene's goddaughter. I've spoken to her on the phone a fair amount, but now that she and her little girl have moved here to Cape Cod, we'll all get to meet them in person soon."

"Where'd they move from?" Nate asked, picking up a Rubik's Cube from the table and giving it an idle twist.

"California." His dad's eyebrows pulled down. "She lost her husband a year and a half ago. I recommended your grief group at the church, but she didn't seem too keen to go…"

"Maybe Hayden and I can go over and introduce ourselves. Did they move somewhere in town?"

"You know the old Sullivan place?"

Nate's eyes popped. "That's not a place, Dad. It's an estate."

His dad shrugged. "I guess her husband had a big life-insurance policy."

Nate nodded as he took a sip of his decaf. Danielle hadn't had any life insurance, although as soon as she'd passed away, Nate had signed up for a policy to make sure Hayden would get the benefits in the event that Nate died, too.

He was glad that the maid of honor's husband had had the foresight to make sure she'd be taken care of financially. From his own personal experience, Nate knew how difficult everything else about navigating life after the death of your spouse could be.

"What's her name?" he asked.

Just as his dad opened his mouth to reply, Nate's cell phone rang.

"Oops, hold that thought," he said, reaching for his phone. He hated to be rude, but as the pastor of Wychmere Community Church, he sometimes got after-hours emergency calls.

Which this appeared to be, since it was the police chief calling.

"Chris," he said, greeting the man on the other end of the line. "What can I do for you?"

"We've got a missing child, Nate, and the mother's distraught. Do you think you could come to the station and sit with her?"

"Of course." Nate shot out of his chair so fast he banged his knee on the table. "Ow."

"Careful there, Pastor," Chief O'Connell said, his voice laced with amusement despite the seriousness of the call. "Don't want you getting in an accident on your way in."

Nate rubbed his knee. "I won't." His clumsiness didn't extend to driving—he'd never been in a car accident in his life. "Do I know them?"

"Probably not—they're new to town. Mom's Amanda Kobayashi. Ivy's the little girl. Not even three years old."

Nate frowned as he searched for his car keys. Those names didn't sound familiar. "How long has the girl been missing?"

Chris sighed. "We're not sure. Mom left her with an elderly babysitter who fell asleep. When she woke up, the girl was gone. Could be hours, could be less."

Lord, let us find her quickly and get her home safe.

He found his keys inside his coat pocket and raced to the front door. "I'll be there as soon as I can."

After he hung up the phone, he called out to let his father know he was leaving. Then he hurried to his car and was about to get in when he heard Hayden yelling from down the street.

"Dad! Dad! Don't leave! Help!"

Nate rushed into the street, squinting into the failing light. It was April on Cape Cod and the temperature was still chilly, although there hadn't been snow on the ground in a month. Hayden was running up from the beach with something bulky in his arms—had something happened to the dog?

No, it wasn't the dog, because Lucy was at Hayden's heels, barking loudly.

Nate ran to meet them. "Hayden, what…?"

Wild-eyed and breathless, Hayden hefted the sodden bundle into Nate's arms. "She was all alone on the jetty, Dad. I think she fell. Her lips are blue, and she's bleeding."

Nate looked down. A rush of adrenaline surged through him as he saw that he was holding a little Asian American girl, right around the age of the missing child. *Oh, thank You, Lord.*

She was unconscious, though, and she was definitely bleeding. In fact, there was so much blood it was running into her eyes.

Hayden shot him a panicked look. "She was crying when I got there, but she passed out when I picked her up. I didn't… I didn't hurt her, did I? I didn't want to move her, but I couldn't leave her. The tide's coming in."

"You did the right thing, champ," Nate said in a calm voice that belied what he was feeling inside. "Get Grandpa. Tell him to call 911. And bring towels!"

His son sprinted to the house, and yelled out, "Grandpa! Grandpa!"

Nate gently laid the girl in the back seat of his car and checked to make sure she was breathing. She was. *Thank You, God.*

A minute later, Hayden and Nate's dad burst onto the front lawn. His father was on the phone, and Hayden's arms were full of dish towels.

Should they wait here for an ambulance? Or head straight to the hospital?

The girl's eyelids fluttered open, and she gave Nate a startled look. "Haybee? Want Haybee!"

"He's right here, sweetheart. He just ran inside to grab you a towel. Don't worry. I'm his dad, and we're going to help you."

The girl started crying, and that decided things for Nate. No sense waiting around for an ambulance when she was hurt and scared.

"Sit in the back, Dad. Give Hayden the phone. You're going to hold her on the ride."

Before his father had time to reply, Hayden yelled, "Get in the car, Grandpa! We have to go!"

"It's okay," Nate said to his son while helping get the girl situated on his father's lap. "Hold her steady, Dad. Don't jostle her head."

"Dad! Dad! Come on! We have to go!"

"Talk to the dispatcher, Hayden. Tell them where you found her." Nate handed his dad a towel. "Hold it on the head wound," he said. "Those bleed a lot, so hopefully it's not as bad as it looks."

His father nodded, determination on his face, and Nate slid into the driver's seat. He closed his eyes for a split second to ground himself. The last thing he needed was shaky hands while he was behind the wheel. *Lord, clear the way for us. Help us get to the hospital quickly so she can get the help she needs.*

Hayden bounced up and down in his seat, clearly too wound up to stay on the phone with 911. "Go, Dad! Go!" Between him and the girl's wailing, it was going to be an eventful ride.

"Hayden, you need to stay calm. It won't help anything to go racing off like chickens with our heads cut off."

"Please, Dad," his son begged. "We can't let her die!"

Nate's heart wrenched as he backed out of the driveway. He didn't think the little girl was going to die, but what did he know? He hadn't thought Danielle was going to die, either, but she'd never even had the chance to meet their son.

"Hold on, champ. Here we go."

* * *

Amanda Kobayashi pushed a strand of blond hair out of her face and blinked at the doctor. "She's really okay?"

The young female physician smiled at her. "Well, like I said, she's got the ten stitches near her hairline, a mild concussion and the broken arm, but give her a few days and she'll be right as rain."

Amanda's knees wobbled and she had to stop herself from lunging forward to envelop the doctor in a giant hug. "You have no idea how much this means to me. Just…thank you so much."

The doctor gave her a kindly pat on the arm. "Get some rest, Mrs. Kobayashi. It's been a long day for you."

Amanda sank into the chair next to Ivy's bed. Her daughter was sleeping peacefully, completely oblivious to the terror she'd caused. Amanda still felt shaky—there was only one other time she'd been that scared in her entire life.

She's safe, Pierce. Our baby's safe.

She was grateful now that she hadn't taken the police chief's advice and called her parents in California. The stress wouldn't have done her dad's high blood pressure any good, and her mother would have already steamrolled her way onto a flight. Worse, she'd probably have called Caroline, too, and cajoled her into driving down from Boston to check on things immediately.

Amanda hadn't spoken to her sister-in-law since before Pierce's funeral. And she certainly didn't want to see her right now.

After stroking Ivy's hair, she rested her hand on her daughter's arm. Ivy had been awake earlier, taking her thumb out of her mouth only long enough to ask for "Haybee," the boy who'd found her on the jetty.

When Amanda had told her she'd get to see him soon,

Ivy had proclaimed, "Haybee my hero," before sticking her thumb back in her mouth and promptly falling asleep.

Amanda felt the exact same way. Apparently, the boy was only twelve years old, but somehow he'd managed to pluck Ivy from the wet, jagged rocks and carry her all the way from the beach to his father's car.

She was already trying to think of ways to repay him. A donation to his college fund, maybe? A bike? A video-game system? Whatever she gave him, it would be too small to convey the depth of her gratitude.

A nurse knocked on the hospital-room door. "Mrs. Kobayashi? The boy who found Ivy's still in the waiting room. Would you like to come out and talk to him?"

"Can you send him in here?" Amanda asked, loath to leave her daughter's side.

"Sure thing. Be right back."

Amanda nodded, then closed her eyes. Now that she knew Ivy was safe and the adrenaline had worn off, she was exhausted.

The nurse knocked again, and Amanda reluctantly opened her eyes. Standing next to the nurse was a studious-looking preteen boy with thick brown hair and glasses. Behind him was a trim, tall man who was cut from the exact same mold, albeit with some gray sprinkled into the hair at his temples. Both of them had their bespectacled blue eyes trained on Ivy.

When the man's gaze skimmed her face, Amanda's breath caught in her throat. He was handsome in a clean-cut, professorial kind of way, but what really snagged her attention was the kindness in his eyes.

For some reason, she felt as though she knew him already—*liked* him already.

You felt that way the first time you saw Pierce, too.

But it wasn't the same. She and Caroline Kobayashi had

been roommates at the University of Massachusetts, and they'd become fast friends almost overnight. By the time Amanda had met Caroline's older brother, Pierce, of course he'd seemed familiar.

And kind.

And safe.

But if the past year and a half had taught her anything, it was that life was unpredictable. Anybody could have the rug ripped out from under them at any time. And the safer you felt, the worse your fall.

Pushing aside the morbid thoughts, Amanda got to her feet. "You must be Hayden," she said, her focus on the boy as she gestured to the bed. "This is Ivy. You were very brave to rescue her, and I—" She fought through her tears to get the rest of her sentence out. "You're our hero, and I can't thank you enough."

The boy blushed and looked down at the floor. "Is she going to be okay?"

Amanda brushed the tears off her face. "They're keeping her here for observation tonight, but the doctor said she should be able to go home tomorrow. She assured me she'll be running all over the place soon enough."

The boy let out a shaky breath. "I was really worried when she passed out."

The man put his hand on the boy's shoulder. "See? Everything's going to be fine." Then he turned his attention to Amanda. "I'm Nate, by the way."

"Amanda, and I'm so grateful to you both."

"God put you in the right place at the right time, didn't He, Hayden?"

The boy nodded. "I couldn't believe it when I heard her crying. I thought it was a cat. Or a joke."

Amanda shook her head. "Just a very curious toddler intent on getting out and exploring the world."

She still didn't understand how Ivy had escaped Joan Weatherbee's house. Had she somehow managed to push open the sliding door in the back?

And speaking of Joan Weatherbee, was the older woman all right? She was pretty sure the police chief had mentioned that she'd been sent to the hospital, too.

Nate pushed his glasses up the bridge of his nose. "I was actually about to head to the police station when Hayden came running up with her. I'm the pastor of Wychmere Community Church, and the police chief asked me to come and wait with you while they searched."

"Did he?" she asked, thinking it was a weird request for the police chief to make. She hadn't been to church since Pierce's funeral, and she had no intention of going back anytime soon, either.

Nate gave her a little smile, and Amanda felt a flutter in her chest, which was…inconvenient. She'd made a decision when Pierce died that she would be like her mother-in-law, Miyoko, and remain faithful to her husband's memory. Loyal to the love they'd shared.

Pierce had lost his father to a heart attack when he was in high school, and Amanda knew that, afterward, he'd held his mother and her devotion to his father's memory in the highest regard.

Amanda would never be as honorable as Miyoko—her thoughts right now proved it—but she could try.

So her focus from here on out was on raising her daughter. Not handsome, scholarly pastors with cute, scholarly sons.

"Part of my ministry is offering prayer and encouragement to people in crisis situations," Nate explained.

"But I'm not part of your congregation."

"'Withhold not good from them to whom it is due, when it is in the power of thine hand to do it.'" Then he looked down at his son. "You know that verse, Hayden?"

The boy nodded. "Proverbs 3:27."

"Whoa." Amanda's eyes went wide. "How did you know that?"

"I memorize a piece of scripture every week. Sometimes two," the boy said proudly.

"Wow." Her gaze caught Nate's and held for a long moment, warmth spreading like molasses through her chest.

Stop making eyes at the pastor!

He smiled again, a dimple popping out on his left cheek, then gave a little shrug. "It just means that we do what we can when we can. Regardless of whether you go to church with us or not."

"That's very…kind of you," she said, feeling touched, but also awkward. She really didn't want to get in to why she didn't go to church anymore with a pastor. She cleared her throat. "Is Joan Weatherbee okay? Chief O'Connell said they had to bring her here, too."

"From what I understand, she's upset, possibly a little disoriented, and they're going to keep her here for a day or two."

Amanda scrubbed at her face. She never should have left Ivy with Mrs. Weatherbee, but she'd been too impatient to wait for a spot to open up at the local day care. When her next-door neighbor had volunteered to babysit for a few hours so Amanda could start training for her new job, Amanda had ignored her internal misgivings and gratefully accepted the help.

A mistake.

A big one.

Almost as big as the mistake Pierce had made that fateful day eighteen months ago.

Amanda snuck a glance at Ivy, whose long brown curls were spread out on her pillow like an unkempt crown. Fortunately, Ivy was safe now. That was the most important thing.

"Is there anything we can get for you before we leave?" Nate asked. "Coffee? Food? A toothbrush?"

"No, no, I'm fine," Amanda said, eyeing the recliner that would serve as her bed tonight. "But thank you."

"All right, then." He and Hayden started for the door, but Nate paused before he exited. "Will your husband need anything? Is he on his way?"

"Oh." Amanda fingered her wedding ring. "No. He passed away when Ivy was just eighteen months old."

"I'm sorry to hear that," Nate said.

Hayden's eyes shot to his dad, then to her. "My mom died when *I* was a baby. My dad still wears his ring, too."

Nate ruffled his son's hair. "I actually run a grief group at the church. You're welcome to join us if you'd like." He took a business card out of his wallet and held it out to her.

Amanda took the card and scanned it. "Wait, your last name is Anderson? Are you related to Bill Anderson?"

Nate blinked in surprise. "Bill's my dad."

Amanda gave her head a little shake. What a small world. "I should have put two and two together when you said you were a pastor."

"Why? How do you know my father?"

"I'm the matron of honor in Bill and Irene's wedding. And you," she said, realizing that they'd be spending a lot more time together over the next few months, "must be the best man."

Chapter Two

Nate had barely pulled the car out of the hospital parking lot when Hayden piped up from the passenger seat. "It's weird that they know Miss Perkins, isn't it? And they're going to be in the wedding! Do you think Ivy and I can walk down the aisle together?"

"I'm sure you can if you want to."

"She won't be scared of me, will she? Because of what happened tonight?" It was way past Hayden's bedtime, but it was clear that his son was all keyed up.

"She's very small, Hayden, so I don't know. But Mrs. Kobayashi said she was asking for you before she fell asleep, so hopefully not."

In his peripheral vision, Nate saw Hayden's chest puff up a little at that information. Good. His son *should* feel proud of himself. Not too proud. But proud.

"I'm proud of you, champ."

Hayden blushed. "It's like you said, Dad. God put me in the right place at the right time."

"Still. Not everyone would have had the courage to do what you did."

"I wasn't going to just leave her there!" Hayden exclaimed, sounding outraged.

"Like I said, bud—you did good."

"Ms. Kobayashi was nice."

"She was," Nate agreed, although *nice* wasn't the first word he'd have used to describe her. With her blond hair, blue eyes and gracefully long limbs, he'd have said she was tall. Elegant. Striking.

A burst of sunshine chasing away the clouds.

But she was also young—much younger than him.

And grieving.

Which, as he well knew, meant there was no way she'd have noticed him the way he'd noticed her.

It had taken him years after Danielle died to even *consider* dating again. Even now, he felt guilty whenever a pretty woman caught his eye.

And, yes, over the last two or three years, he'd gone on a few dates to appease the matchmaking ladies in his congregation, but never with anyone he'd felt an actual connection to.

Until now.

Although, of course, he hadn't been on a date with Amanda Kobayashi. He'd literally just met the woman.

In his heart of hearts, he had to admit that he did want to find love again. He'd like to find someone who'd be a good stepmother to Hayden and who might even want to have another baby or two.

But the thought of having more children always stopped him cold. He and Danielle had wanted a big family, but with God's help, he'd learned to be content with what he had.

"I wonder if she'd let me babysit Ivy," Hayden mused. He'd been trying to think of ways to make money for several months now. He was hoping to go to a chess tournament in Florida near Walt Disney World with his chess club over the summer and, of course, the trip would be pricey. Nate had told him that if he could save enough money for the plane tickets, Nate would cover the rest of it.

Just one of the many reasons you need to go back to school and get that PhD.

Being a small-town pastor had a lot of perks, but a generous salary wasn't one of them. He'd done all right providing for Hayden up to this point, but as his son hit the teenage years, the costs of child-rearing would only increase. Not to mention saving for college.

But if Nate got his PhD from Harvard Divinity School, he'd be a religious studies professor by the time Hayden was ready to apply to university. And, as he knew from his time with Danielle, many colleges and universities offered free tuition to their professors' children.

Or, if not free, subsidized by as much as 90 percent.

"Babysitting's a lot of responsibility," he said evenly.

"I can handle it, Dad. I could even take that babysitting class at the community center!"

Surprised, Nate threw a quick glance at his son. "You want to take a babysitting class?"

"Julie said she makes eighteen dollars an hour babysitting those twins down the street. Eighteen dollars an *hour.*"

Nate nodded, trying to keep the smile off his face. His son liked to be taken seriously. "That's good money." In his quest to fund his trip, Hayden had done some snow shoveling, dog walking and yard work around the neighborhood, but those jobs all paid significantly less than eighteen bucks an hour.

Hayden cleaned his glasses on his shirt and unceremoniously stuck them back on his face. "It's *great* money."

"That's for twins, though. Ivy's an only child." He was glad for that. Hayden would surely have had his hands full with little Derrick and Dylan Williams.

"I wouldn't ask Ms. Kobayashi for that much. I'm just saying, that's all."

"Ah," Nate said, his lips twitching. "You're just saying."

"Yes, Dad," Hayden replied, sounding every inch the ex-asperated tween. "If I took the class maybe I could find more babysitting clients. Especially if Ms. Kobayashi lets me watch Ivy and gives me a good recommendation."

"That's not a bad idea, champ."

"Ivy's cute. I could take her to the park and stuff."

"She's cute," Nate conceded, "but don't forget that she's feisty. She managed to sneak out of Mrs. Weatherbee's house and make her way out onto the jetty."

"Yeah, but Mrs. Weatherbee's old. I'm young and have lots of energy."

Again, Nate fought to keep the smile off his face. "You *are* quite energetic."

"We could do crafts, I could read her stories, maybe I could even teach her how to play chess!"

"She's pretty young for chess."

Hayden scrunched his nose. "Checkers, then. I'll teach her how to play checkers."

"Good plan." Nate pulled into his driveway and turned off the engine, suddenly feeling bone-weary. He scrubbed a hand over his face. Starting with the acceptance email from Harvard this morning, it had been a long, emotional roller coaster of a day.

And he had no doubt that his father would want to debrief after Hayden went to bed. Which would probably lead to Nate spilling the beans about Harvard. And then who knew how late it would be before he got to go to sleep?

Hayden opened his car door but hesitated before stepping out. "I'll ask her next week at dinner, okay?"

"About checkers?"

"No, Dad," Hayden said, sighing with exaggerated patience. "About babysitting."

"Oh, right. Sure. You can ask." If they even had dinner together, that was. Irene had breezed into Ivy's hospital room just after they'd discovered that they were all going to be in the wedding together, then dropped a dinner invitation into their laps before breezing back out and taking Nate's dad with her.

Nate gave his son a steely look. "But don't push it if she says no. I wouldn't be surprised if she wants to keep an eye on Ivy herself for a while."

"'Kay." His son opened the door and hopped out of the car. "You coming?"

Nate shook his head. "I need a few minutes. You go see if Grandpa's home yet." Although he and Hayden had left the hospital around the same time as Irene, she was notorious for having a lead foot, and he'd be astonished if they'd beat his father home.

Hayden nodded and hurried toward the house. Nate closed his eyes for a quick moment of quiet time. No matter how much the whole Harvard thing was weighing on him, the important thing today was that a child had been in danger and now she was safe.

Thank You, Lord, for sending Hayden out for that walk at exactly the right time. Thank You for protecting that little girl from harm.

He twisted his wedding ring around on his finger, remembering the day twelve years ago when his clumsiness meant he hadn't been in the right place at the right time. When he hadn't asked the right questions or pushed the doctors hard enough. When God hadn't protected his wife from harm.

Lord, help me trust in You.

He got out of the car and went inside, where his father was

listening to a bright-eyed Hayden regale him—again—with the story of Ivy's rescue from the rocks.

When Hayden was done, Nate said, "Why don't you go get ready for bed?"

"I haven't done my homework yet."

"It's late. I'll email your teachers. This is one instance where I think you'll get a pass."

Hayden's eyes popped. "Wow. Thanks!" Then he high-tailed it up the stairs before Nate could change his mind.

Nate's father turned to him, eyes dancing. "Quite a night, eh?"

Nate sighed. "All's well that ends well. But you really had no idea that little girl was Ivy?"

"I'm sorry, son. I'd never met her before—only ever seen a picture. Plus, it was dark, and there was a lot of blood. I didn't know it was her until Irene showed up and filled me in."

Made sense, but it was still quite the coincidence. Nate lowered himself onto the plaid family room couch...right on top of one of the Rubik's Cubes he'd been trying to solve. "Ouch."

He set the Cube on the coffee table, annoyed with himself for leaving it out in the first place. He had several, and he was always losing them around the house. "So...were you going to tell me about this dinner Irene's planning?"

His father held up his hands and gave him a sheepish grin. "You know Irene."

Nate groaned. "Please tell me this isn't one of her match-making schemes."

His father was sitting in the overstuffed easy chair across from the couch. The small, three-bedroom cottage was the same house Nate had grown up in, and the furniture showed its age. "Would it be so bad if it was?"

Nate pinned his father with a stare. "Dad."

His father stared right back. "Nathaniel."

"She's way too young for me. If she's thirty, I'll be shocked."

"She's twenty-six."

Nate's jaw dropped. "You thought Dani was too young for me, and we were only five years apart."

His father waved that off. "Dani was a sophomore in college when you met her. Amanda's a full-fledged adult with a child of her own. It's different."

"It's not that different," Nate insisted, wondering what his parishioners would have to say if he started dating someone thirteen years his junior. "Plus, she's a widow."

His dad gave him a funny look. "So are you."

"She's a *recent* widow."

"Not everyone waits over a decade to start dating again."

Nate pushed a hand through his hair. "This isn't a good time."

His dad stroked his mustache. "It's never a good time, and I understand that, believe me, but—"

"No, Dad, you don't understand. I applied to the PhD program at Harvard Divinity School, and I just found out this morning that I got in."

His dad went still. "You got in. To Harvard."

"Classes start at the end of August."

"You never told me you were applying to grad school."

Nate dropped his elbows to his knees and leaned forward. "It's something Dani and I talked about. Tim thinks it'll be good for me, too."

His father sat back and steepled his fingers. "Ah. Did Tim write you a reference?"

"Yes." Tim Ellsworth had been Nate's adviser while he was getting his master's degree. He was also his father-in-law, and he'd always been supportive of Nate, even after Danielle had passed away.

When Nate was feeling burned-out—which was a lot more often these days than it used to be—Tim was the person he talked to. Tim had been a pastor before he became a professor, so he knew what it was like to be needed by so many people on a regular basis…and truly known and supported by so few.

According to Tim, the academic lifestyle was more balanced. There were classes to teach and students to mentor and papers to grade—lots and lots of papers to grade—but at the end of the day, you could unplug. Unwind. Recharge. No after-hours crisis calls or church volunteers who needed to vent or visits with older congregants who lived alone and didn't see anyone else during the week.

When Nate had first started out in his ministry, Danielle had been right there by his side, helping him carry the mental and emotional load that came with the job. Ever since the pandemic, that load had gotten heavier, and he was getting awfully tired of shouldering it all alone.

"Dani would be proud of you, son," his father said. "But are you sure this is the right move for you *now*?"

"I got a merit scholarship, Dad. It covers the full cost of tuition plus a stipend for living expenses, which'll be helpful since the cost of living in the Boston area is so high. And now that Hayden's getting older…"

"Have you told him?"

"Not yet."

"He's not going to be happy."

Nate picked up the Rubik's Cube and fiddled with it. "He will be in ten years when he graduates from college without huge student loans."

His dad crinkled his brow. "How do you figure?"

"Professors' kids get free tuition at a lot of schools."

"Ah," his father said again. "Like Danielle. But what if he doesn't want to go to college where you're teaching?"

Nate gave a little shrug. "Professors make a lot more money than pastors."

His dad's mustache twitched in disappointment. "Nate."

But Nate wasn't in the mood to hear it. "Dad."

"What about your congregation?"

"They can find a new pastor. This sort of thing happens all the time."

"Not here, it doesn't. Before you, we had Pastor Sam, and he served for more than forty years."

Nate sighed. His dad was a baby boomer who'd taught chemistry at the same public high school for his entire career. He didn't understand that millennials just didn't operate the same way.

Not that Nate was a job hopper. No, he'd been happy at Wychmere Community Church for the past twelve years. But his son came first. Always.

"I know, but this was never the long-term plan."

"Sometimes plans change," his father said.

"And sometimes they don't."

His dad sighed. "Well, Irene's going to be disappointed."

Nate fiddled some more with the Rubik's Cube, but he was just making it worse. "We're not leaving until after the wedding."

"Not about the wedding. About Amanda."

Nate smirked and set the Cube back on the coffee table. "I knew she was up to something."

"We just want you to be happy."

"I am happy, Dad."

His father gave him a searching look. "Are you?"

"Yes," he replied, but for some reason, the word felt like wet cotton in his mouth.

* * *

Amanda unclipped Ivy from her car seat, thankful that her soon-to-be three-year-old daughter hadn't yet figured out how to undo the straps herself. Then she glanced over at the Candy Shack and took a deep breath. Why was she so nervous? It was just dinner with her godmother and a few new friends.

"Candy, Mama? Please, please, please?" Dressed in yellow tights, a pink tutu and a *Sesame Street* sweatshirt, Ivy pouted, shooting longing looks at the Candy Shack's window display, where giant swirl lollipops had been set up to look like a spring flower garden: cheerful and bright.

"No, chickadee. You can have dessert after dinner."

"With Haybee?"

Amanda nodded. Ivy had been talking about Hayden nonstop since she'd gotten out of the hospital last week. "Hayden will be there."

She and Ivy had gone shopping this morning and picked up a set of lawn darts for the boy. Amanda knew it wasn't enough, but it was a start. Hopefully, he'd like it.

Holding the lawn darts in one hand, she took firm hold of Ivy's hand with the other and walked around the side of the Candy Shack to the set of outdoor stairs up to Irene's apartment. They ascended, then knocked on the door.

Irene flung it open with her usual vim and vigor. "Amanda, sweetheart, so good to see you!" She leaned in to give Amanda a quick, perfumed hug, then turned her attention to Ivy. "And you, young lady! You sure are good at keeping us all on our toes, aren't you?"

Ivy looked at her feet. "I hab toes. Ten toes."

"That's right," Irene said, "and ten fingers, too."

Ivy wiggled her fingers, then stuck her thumb in her mouth, managing to ingest some of her hair with it, too.

"Come in, come in," Irene said, ushering them into her living room, where Bill, Nate and Hayden rose from their seats when the women walked into the room. *Good manners must run in the family*, Amanda thought. *How sweet.*

Ivy pulled her thumb out of her mouth with a pop and ran over to Hayden. "Haybee! Haybee! I cast!" She held up her broken arm for him to see.

"Wow, Ivy, what a cool cast! Can I draw a picture on it for you?"

Ivy's eyes lit up. "A picture, Mama! He draw me a picture!"

Hayden looked to Amanda. "Is that okay, Ms. Kobayashi?"

"Of course, honey. You can draw whatever you want."

He angled his gaze back to Ivy. "Do you like flowers?"

"Fowlers are pretty!" her daughter squealed, mangling the pronunciation of the word, as always.

"Do you have any markers, Miss Perkins?"

Irene touched her short, white perm. "I'm going to be your grandma, Hayden. You can call me Irene."

The boy blushed. "Okay. Irene."

"And, yes, you can check my kitchen drawer."

"Come on, Ivy." Hayden held out his hand. "Let's go see what color flowers you want."

Ivy glommed on to his hand and practically pranced into the kitchen next to him.

"Uh-oh," Amanda said, shooting Nate an apologetic look. "I hope he doesn't mind having a little shadow tonight."

Nate gave her a reassuring smile. "He was looking forward to seeing her. He won't mind."

Amanda breathed a sigh of relief, then held up the bag that contained the lawn darts. "We brought him a present."

"You didn't have to do that."

"I hope he likes lawn darts."

Nate's smile widened, his dimple making another appearance and setting off a round of flutters in Amanda's chest. "I'm sure he'll love them."

"Want some crackers and cheese, dear?" Irene asked, holding out a platter and interrupting Amanda's train of thought.

She helped herself to a piece of cheddar and a couple of grapes. Irene's living room was just as she remembered: cleaned within an inch of its life, but cozy, too. There were china figurines on the mantel and framed photos of Irene and her copious friends and acquaintances clustered on the walls.

"The little one seems to be doing okay now," Bill commented, stacking his paper plate full of cheese while motioning toward the kitchen with his mustache.

Amanda huffed out a rueful laugh. "She's fine. I'm the one who's traumatized."

"There, there, don't you fret," Irene said briskly. "Kids are resilient."

"She's always sneaking off somewhere, and then I went and moved us to the beach!" You'd think that after her husband had drowned, Amanda would have been afraid to live by the water, but she hadn't been. Not until last week.

"Do they know how she got out of Joan's house?" Nate asked.

Amanda set down her plate on the coffee table. "Best guess is she squeezed herself through the little cat entrance in the side door."

Bill's eyebrows pinched together. "And where was Joan when all this was happening?"

Amanda sighed. "She fell asleep in front of the TV."

"Well, listen," Irene said. "If you need a babysitter, you just bring Ivy right over here. I don't have a TV *or* a cat door, so you know she'll be safe with me."

Amanda cast her godmother a wry look. "I thought the whole point of me moving down here was so you can retire. Not trade jobs with me."

Nate's gaze moved back and forth between the two women. "You're retiring, Irene?"

The older woman fluffed her perm. "After the wedding, you know your father and I want to travel."

"Well, sure," Nate said. "But—"

"And Amanda here was looking for a new challenge. It's a perfect fit."

"Except for the whole my-daughter-is-a-tiny-escape-artist thing," Amanda added, trying to play it off as funny by rolling her eyes. The truth was, though, that she was stumped. She'd have to put off learning the ropes at the Candy Shack until a spot opened up at the day care for Ivy.

Which, unfortunately, might not be until the fall.

Amanda didn't want to wait that long to start her new job. Her sole aim in moving to Cape Cod had been to establish her independence. She'd married Pierce, an up-and-coming young dentist, less than a month after her college graduation, and although she'd worked part-time as a receptionist in his dental office before she'd had Ivy, she'd never held a full-time job.

Growing up, she'd been the youngest of six siblings…and the only girl. She'd been the apple of her father's eye and the sole focus of all her mother's vicarious aspirations. And after she'd moved to Massachusetts to carve out a life for herself away from her mother's machinations, she'd gotten engaged at nineteen to a twenty-nine-year-old man.

She'd loved Pierce desperately and didn't regret a thing, but it was hard to take yourself seriously when you were a wealthy twenty-six-year-old widow who hadn't earned a dime of the money in your bank account for yourself.

It was also hard to convince your mother to stop trying to get you to move back home.

She drummed her fingers on the arm of her chair. "Maybe I should look for an honest-to-goodness nanny…" Although having a nanny had never been something she'd wanted for her child.

Day care was one thing. There were multiple teachers there to care for the kids, and lots of little friends to socialize with. A nanny was a smidgen too close to a replacement mom for Amanda's comfort.

What she'd *really* like was a flexible job she could bring Ivy to—one with childcare on-site.

But unless she relocated, retrained and somehow worked her way into a *Fortune* 500 company, the chances of that happening were slim to none.

And even if she somehow found the perfect job situation, her mother *still* wouldn't give up hope that she could convince Amanda and Ivy to come back to California if she just kept nagging.

"Hayden will do it," Nate said. "He can babysit for you. At least after school, until you find someone permanent."

Amanda turned to stare at him. He seemed serious, but maybe he had a deadpan sense of humor like his dad. She gave a little laugh. "I'm sure he has other things he'd rather be doing."

Nate spread his hands. "He's trying to save up for a chess tournament near Disney World. He's the one who brought it up."

Amanda knitted her brow. It was a sweet offer, but… "Has he ever babysat before?"

"He's hoping you can serve as a reference."

She blew a strand of hair out of her eye. She didn't want to offend the guy, but she also didn't want to leave her daughter with an inexperienced young boy. "Um... I don't know..."

"Nonsense," Irene said. "Bring them both over here. Hayden can do the heavy lifting, and Bill or I will keep an eye on them while you're at the store."

"Oh," Amanda said, "I couldn't ask you to spend all that time supervising them..."

Irene turned to her fiancé. "You're only over at the high school twice a week for chess club this spring, so you'll be around Monday, Wednesday and Friday afternoons, won't you?"

Bill winked at Amanda, then said, "Yes, dear" to Irene.

Irene put her hands on her hips. "Oh, don't you 'yes, dear' me. You know you won't have to lift a finger if Hayden's on the case. You can just sit here and read the paper."

Bill laughed and held up his hands. "I said yes already! No need to get testy."

Irene smirked. "This isn't testy, ducky, it's feisty."

"And I love you for it," Bill said, leaning over and giving her a kiss on the cheek.

Amanda blushed and looked away. Pierce had never been big on public displays of affection. His parents were immigrants from Japan, where PDA was generally taboo. Add that to the fact that Amanda's older brothers had yelled "Mush!" every time anything even slightly romantic had come on TV while she was growing up, and Amanda had never been all that comfortable with PDA herself.

She turned to Nate. "Well, I guess it would be okay, if he really wants to babysit..."

"He really wants to."

"Perfect," Irene proclaimed, giving her hands a brisk clap. "That will give you two time to do some wedding-related errands for us, too."

"Sure," Amanda said.

"Great, because I enrolled you in dance lessons at All That Jazz on Main Street. I know you're a good dancer, Amanda, but Nate has two left feet, and we want the two of you to join us for the first dance at the wedding. Can't have him falling on his face in front of everyone. Or, worse yet, breaking one of your toes."

Nate frowned. "Really, Irene? Did you have to bring that up?"

Amanda gaped at him. "Did you literally break someone's toe?"

His face went red with embarrassment. "It was decades ago at the junior prom. I was sixteen."

She couldn't help laughing. "Oh, you poor thing!"

One corner of his mouth quirked up. "Believe me, I wasn't the one anyone was worried about back then."

"I'm sure you weren't. Was she your girlfriend?"

"Not after that."

Amanda tried to stifle her laughter, but she couldn't hold it back. "Should I wear steel-toed boots to our lessons?"

"Didn't I just give you a good enough reason to back out?"

She shrugged. "I like a challenge."

Their gazes locked, her words hanging in the air for a good five seconds. *Oh, my.* She hoped that hadn't sounded as suggestive to his ears as it had to hers. *Stop flirting with the pastor!*

Irene clapped her hands again. "Well, dear, you have your work cut out for you. Better get going. First lesson starts in thirty-five minutes."

Amanda's mouth fell open. "The lessons start tonight?"

"Dad, Irene, this really isn't—" Nate began.

"Off you go," Irene insisted, on her feet and collecting

their cheese plates. "Ellen's expecting you. Don't keep her waiting."

Flabbergasted, Amanda looked back and forth between Irene and Bill. "But I thought we were all having dinner?"

"All That Jazz is right next to the pizza parlor," Irene said smoothly. "You two can grab something quick beforehand, or something more leisurely after."

Amanda pressed her lips into a thin line. "And the kids?"

"We've got takeout from the Barnacle Bakery arriving in about—" Irene checked her watch "—five minutes. A burger for Hayden and chicken nuggets for little Miss Ivy. Now, go. Scoot. Ellen doesn't like it when her students are late."

Speechless, Amanda looked to Nate, who lifted his eyebrows as if to say "it's up to you."

"Let me go check on Ivy," she said slowly. This whole thing was a little strange, but if her godmother needed her to help Nate become a better dancer, Amanda would do it. She owed Irene a lot. Who else would let an untested single mom train to take on the manager's job at a well-established store? And with Bill, Irene and Hayden here, it would be hard for Ivy to get into any trouble.

She went into the kitchen, where Ivy sat kicking her feet under the table, while Hayden drew a colorful bouquet on her cast. "Mommy has to go out for a little bit, chickadee. Do you want to come with me or stay here for dinner with Auntie Irene and Uncle Bill? They're getting you chicken nuggets."

"You stay, Haybee?" the girl asked.

"I'm staying," he confirmed, intent on his drawing.

"Me, too," she said, hearts in her eyes. "I stay with you."

Chapter Three

Nate opened the car door for Amanda. "Are you sure you want to do this? I can go back inside and tell them no."

She slid into the seat. "You've met Irene, right?" she asked, tucking a strand of blond hair behind her ear. "When she gets an idea in her head, she doesn't take no for an answer. And besides, if Hayden really does want to babysit, this will be a good test run."

"That's true," he said, then shut her door and came around to the driver's side. He reminded her a lot of Pierce, whose manners had always been on point. "But I don't like the way they bullied us into it."

"Well, if you can't bully your maid of honor and best man into doing things for you, who can you bully?" she joked.

He started the car. It was older, but it was clean and well maintained. Before he reversed out of the driveway, though, he turned to her. "You do realize they're trying to set us up, don't you?"

Amanda gasped. *She wouldn't!*

But this was Irene they were talking about. She would.

"She knows I'm not looking to date again. And even if I was…" She waved her hand toward Nate, then stopped herself before finishing her thought. She doubted he wanted to hear that he was too old for her. Obviously, she liked older men, but if she ever dipped her toes back into the dating pool, she'd stick with guys closer to her own age.

If she didn't, her family would never let her live it down. Her mother, especially, would be insufferable. She'd *loved* the fact that Amanda had married Pierce straight out of college. "With a man like that to take care of you," she'd proclaimed gleefully after he proposed, "you'll never have to work a day in your life!"

Which was in no way, shape or form why Amanda had married him, but her mother didn't care. To her, marriage was more about securing a certain kind of lifestyle than it was about love.

But Amanda wasn't getting married again, anyway, so her mother's thoughts on the matter were moot.

"Hate to break it to you," Nate said, his dimple winking at her as he pulled onto the road, "but my dad all but admitted their matchmaking plans to me. I thought I talked him down by telling him I'm moving to Boston in the fall, but apparently not."

"Oh, man," Amanda groaned. "I'm sorry she dragged your dad into her scheming. They're going to be *so* disappointed."

He chuckled. "It'll serve them right, though."

"It sure will." She relaxed into her seat. Thank goodness they were on the same page about not dating. Otherwise, this whole matron-of-honor-and-best-man thing could get awkward fast. "So why are you moving to Boston?"

"Getting a PhD."

"Ooh, awesome. In what?"

"Theology."

She laughed again. "Of course. Silly me. What school?"

"Harvard."

"Ooh la la. Smarty-pants."

He cracked a grin at that, and she was glad. People didn't

always appreciate her goofy streak, and it was nice to know that she didn't have to hide that part of herself around him.

"What about you?" he asked. "I didn't know Irene was looking to retire."

"I don't think she was. Not until I told her I wanted to move back to Massachusetts and find a real job."

"So you lived in our great state before?"

She nodded. "I went to college here. Well, not *here* here. Western Massachusetts. Amherst."

"Ah," he said. "UMass?"

"Mmm-hmm. And my husband grew up in one of the Boston suburbs. We moved there after we got married." Two streets over from his mother. And once Caroline got married, she and her husband had lived within walking distance, too.

One big, happy family.

Until they weren't.

Amanda sighed. She was still so angry with Caroline, even though she knew it wasn't good for her mental health. But she didn't know what to do about it.

Therapy hadn't helped, expressing it by punching pillows hadn't helped and she wasn't talking to God these days, so praying about it was out.

Which left…avoidance. Running away.

"And then you moved to California?" Nate asked.

"I grew up in California. I went back home after he died."

"I did the same thing when my wife died. Came back here from Texas."

The two of them had a lot in common. Amanda didn't know many young widows or widowers, and it was nice to talk to someone who understood where she was coming from. "And you've lived with your dad all this time?"

"My mom was still around for the first couple of years,

which was a big help. But since then, yep—me, my dad and Hayden. The three musketeers."

"That's great. My mom and I… I mean, she just kind of swooped in and spirited me and Ivy back to California after my husband died. I was in a pretty bad fog for a while, so I'm glad she did it, but once I started coming out of it and wanted to do more for myself and Ivy, she had a hard time letting go, you know?"

"My mother-in-law slapped me in the face when I told her I was moving back to Cape Cod with Hayden. So, yeah, I get that it can be hard for grandmas to let go."

Amanda's mouth fell open. "She slapped you? Seriously?"

Nate sighed. "Dani and I married young. She was only twenty-one when she got pregnant, and when she died during the pregnancy, her mom blamed me. When I moved back here with Hayden, she took it personally. Like I was taking the last piece of her baby girl away from her."

"That's terrible. I'm really sorry." Although Amanda was burning with curiosity about what had happened to his wife, there was no way she was going to ask. She hated it when people asked that of her.

She'd much rather talk about the person Pierce had been than the circumstances surrounding his death.

She felt bad for Nate and his mother-in-law, but truly awful for Dani. At least Pierce had had almost a year and a half with Ivy. He'd been so proud and happy to be a dad. Nate's wife had never even had a chance to experience the joy of being a parent.

"We managed to smooth things over," Nate said. "She and my father-in-law visit all the time."

"That's good." Amanda loved her mother-in-law, Miyoko. But since seeing Miyoko meant seeing Caroline, Amanda hadn't visited since she'd come back to Massachusetts.

After a moment, Nate pulled up in front of All That Jazz, which was nestled between an art gallery and a souvenir shop that stocked sand-dollar necklaces, stylish sun hats and monogrammed beach bags. Franco's, the popular pizza joint Irene had mentioned, was next to that.

Nate nodded his chin at the pizzeria. "Want to eat first or wait until after?"

"After. Unless you're hungry now?"

"No, after's good. I might have to buy you dinner to apologize for what I'm about to put you through."

Amanda laughed. "It won't be that bad."

Nate smirked. "Your feet might not agree with that assessment."

Ellen Langley, the dance instructor, stopped clapping out the beat. "Nate! Eyes off the floor!"

He looked up, but it threw him off the rhythm of the box step he and Amanda were practicing, and he stumbled. Again.

This just got more and more embarrassing.

The dance studio wasn't huge, but it had full-length mirrors along the entire back wall, so he'd had a first-class view of himself fumbling through the waltz all night.

It was clear that Amanda was well-versed in ballroom dancing, which made him feel even worse. If he wasn't such a terrible partner, she probably wouldn't need any lessons at all.

"I'm sorry," he said for the umpteenth time that night.

Amanda gave his hand a reassuring squeeze. "It just takes practice. You'll get it."

"Before I permanently disfigure your feet?"

She laughed, and the movement made her silky hair swish over his hand, which was resting lightly on her back. The scent of coconut tickled his nose.

He swallowed hard. He hadn't held a woman this close for this long in years.

She was the perfect height for him, too—just a few inches shorter than his six feet. Graceful. Kind. Able to roll with his clumsiness and keep laughing about it.

He let go of her abruptly. *She's only twenty-six*, he reminded himself, *and she's not looking to date.* "I think we've had enough torture for one night, Ellen."

Ellen sighed. He'd heard she was looking to sell the studio, and if her attitude was any indication, she'd like to do it sooner rather than later. "Practice at home before next week, Nate. We've got our work cut out for us."

He gave her a good-natured wink. "Don't I know it."

He helped Amanda put on her coat, then pushed open the door to the street. "Tell me the truth. Will pizza really make up for that debacle?"

"Hmm." She tapped her chin with her pointer finger, pretending to consider it. "A slice or a whole pie?"

"A whole pie, obviously."

"Unlimited toppings?"

"Absolutely."

"Then it definitely makes up for it."

"I'm sorry. I tried to warn you."

"Nate." She put her hand on his forearm. "It's really okay."

"I didn't hurt you?"

She looked up at him through her long lashes. Even in the lamplight, her eyes were a rich, cornflower blue. "Not even a little."

He let out a sigh of relief as he held open the door to Franco's. He'd hate it if he'd injured her.

She pulled her cell phone out of her pocket. "Why don't you go in and order? I'm just going to call Irene really quick and check on Ivy."

He nodded and went inside. Franco's was always popular, but the place was packed tonight. Kids squealed as they played arcade games in the corner, and conversation burbled from the tables, where families and friends sat to eat their pizzas, wings and French fries.

Nate nodded and said hello to a few people he knew, then got in line at the counter, scanning the chalkboard menu overhead. There was a blueberry ricotta pizza on the specials menu tonight, complete with mozzarella, caramelized onions, basil and a honey drizzle. Nate's mouth watered. That sounded phenomenal.

The bell over the door jangled, and Amanda joined him in line, bringing a hint of the cool night air inside with her. "How's Ivy doing?" he asked.

"So far, so good. Irene said Hayden's teaching her how to play checkers."

Nate chuckled. "Oh, yeah. He mentioned he wanted to do that."

"Did you see the sign in the window of the dance studio?"

"What sign?"

"Is it really for sale?"

"Yes." He cocked his head to the side. "Why? Are you interested?"

"Just curious."

But he'd seen the spark of enthusiasm in her eyes. "You'd make a great dance teacher. You've got a lot of patience."

She laughed and looked up at the menu. "What's good here?"

"I'm eyeing the blueberry ricotta," he said, pointing to the list of personal pan pizzas on the board.

"Whoa, sounds…interesting."

"I'll share a piece if you want to try it."

"Sure. I like pineapple on my pizza, so why not?"

"What else should we get?"

She studied the chalkboard. "How about the Mediterranean? Feta and olives. Yum."

"Coming right up," he told her, then placed the order. When an older couple got up from a booth in the back, Amanda darted over and started wiping it down with a napkin.

"Way to snag a table," Nate said, taking off his jacket and draping it over the back of his chair.

"I'm speedy like that."

"Did you and your husband go dancing a lot? You're way better than I am."

She smiled. "No, that's all thanks to cotillion."

He gave her a quizzical look. "I thought you grew up in California. Isn't cotillion a Southern thing?"

"It might be more prevalent in the South, but we had it in Los Angeles, too."

"LA, huh? Do you know any movie stars?"

"Um…" She blushed. "Yes."

"Oh." Nate sat up straighter. She was fascinating. "I was teasing, but do tell."

"My dad's an entertainment lawyer. A lot of his clients are famous."

"Did you live in Hollywood?"

She shook her head. "Palos Verdes. It's about forty-five minutes south of downtown LA, depending on traffic."

"Is the traffic in LA as bad as everyone says?"

"It's bad, but no worse than Boston."

He shuddered at the thought of Boston traffic, which was absolutely brutal. "If you grew up in LA rubbing elbows with the rich and famous, what made you decide to go to college in Western Massachusetts?"

She laughed. "I met a few actors and actresses at my dad's

firm's Christmas parties, but I wouldn't say I was 'rubbing elbows' with them. And as for Western Massachusetts, it was pretty much the farthest I could get away from my family without leaving the country."

"Uh-oh," he said. "Trouble at home?"

She tipped her head to the side. "Not trouble, exactly, but I'm the youngest of six. And the only girl."

"Five older brothers? Oh, boy."

She grinned. "You can say that again."

"Do you not get along with your brothers?"

"I get along with my brothers just fine. It's my mom who drives me batty."

"Ah."

"She means well. But she…drinks sometimes. Dealing with her can be…challenging."

"I'm sorry." Nate had counseled enough family members of alcoholics to know the kind of havoc uncontrolled drinking could cause.

Amanda lifted her shoulder. "She's not all bad. But even when she's not drinking, she has some very strong opinions about things. Me, especially. My brothers just laugh her off when she tries to get on them about anything, but for me…" She bit her lip. "It's better when I have some space."

From the counter, Franco called out their order number. Nate got up to grab their pizzas, while Amanda picked up their drinks, straws, napkins and a couple of paper plates.

"Do you want to say the blessing, or should I do the honors?" he asked.

A flash of reluctance flickered across her face. "You go ahead."

He decided to keep it short and simple. "Lord, bless this food and the hands that made it. Amen."

"Amen," she echoed softly.

He opened the pizza boxes and motioned for Amanda to choose first. She took one slice of each pie, and then he helped himself.

After taking a giant bite of the blueberry ricotta pizza—which was sweet and delicious—and washing it down with a mouthful of Sprite, he said, "In the hospital, you mentioned that you're not part of my congregation. Have you found another church you like?"

She rolled the paper wrapper from her straw into a little ball. "Not yet."

"Do you want some recommendations?"

She ducked her head. "I'm not really looking right now."

Something inside his chest dipped with disappointment at that, which was silly. They'd already established that neither of them was interested in dating. He had no business feeling let down by her lack of faith.

"Okay." He didn't shy away from sharing the gospel, but he also believed that, as Ecclesiastes 3:7 said, there was "a time to keep silence, and a time to speak." Patience, he'd learned over his years as a pastor, often went a long, long way.

He ate some more pizza, then said, "Tell me about your husband. What was his name?"

Surprised, Amanda looked up from her little paper ball. "You want to talk about Pierce?"

"That's a good name. Pierce. Very masculine."

"That was his American name. His parents are Japanese. They called him Yori at home."

"Oh, interesting." He could tell by the way her posture had straightened that she liked talking about him—the same way he liked talking about Danielle. Not about her death or its aftermath, but about the beautiful, caring person he'd fallen in love with. The one he'd miss until the day he died. "What did you call him?"

"Pierce. That's what he liked to be called. Yori was like a nickname that only his parents used."

"Did he grow up here or in Japan?"

"Here. His parents moved before he was born. He was American."

"How'd you meet?"

She smiled. "He was my best friend's older brother."

"Ah, classic."

"How'd you meet your wife?"

"She was my academic adviser's daughter."

Her eyebrows shot up. "Really? Did he introduce you or…?"

He gave a short laugh. "He did. He thought we might hit it off."

"He must have thought very highly of you."

"Or he just knew that his daughter had a type. Awkward academics."

"Come on now," she said, giving his arm a little swat. "You're not awkward."

"Your feet would beg to disagree."

"Why don't we set up some time to practice together before the next lesson? You've clearly got a complex about dancing."

Nate choked on a laugh. "You want to give me *more* opportunities to crush your toes?"

She shook her head, smiling. "I want to give you the opportunity to feel confident about your ability to waltz before the wedding."

"That's a very generous offer, but we've got time, right?" he hedged, worried about spending time with her outside the dance studio. "There's still more than two months until the big day."

If the way he'd reacted to holding her earlier was any indication, it wouldn't be a good idea to dance with her one-on-one. He wasn't looking to start a relationship right before he moved, but he wasn't above temptation—*the flesh is weak* and all of that.

Why put himself in a shaky situation with a woman who was thirteen years younger than him, uninterested in dating *and* uncertain about her faith? Even if she was kind, and easygoing, and easy on the eyes…

"What other wedding-related 'errands' do you think Irene's going to send us on?" Amanda asked.

He swallowed another bite of pizza. "Well, I heard her telling my dad that she wants a coed wedding shower, so that'll probably be on the list."

"Oh, yup. She already told me I'm in charge of that."

"If you need help, feel free to rope me in."

"Thanks, but I think I've got it covered. Already got a theme and everything." She put her hands up as though she was displaying her theme in lights. "'Taco 'Bout Love.'"

Nate chuckled. "Going to serve tacos, I'm guessing?"

"Of course."

"Then it's perfect."

She smiled. "Thank you. In that case, I'm going to order the decorations as soon as I get home."

"Well, if I can't help you with that, I'm sure she'll think of a bunch of other odd jobs for us to do together."

Amanda sighed. "Probably."

The bell above the door jangled, and Brett Richardson, a congregant whom Nate also considered a friend, walked in. "Nate! Fancy meeting you here," he said, clapping Nate on the shoulder.

"Hey, buddy. What's new?"

"Not much. Just grabbing some dinner for Valerie and the boys." Brett had been dating Valerie Williams, who was the guardian of her three-year-old twin brothers, for the last six months. "What's new with *you*?" he added, tossing Nate a pointed glance before throwing a smile at Amanda.

Nate stiffened. Brett was head over heels for Valerie, but he was a good-looking guy. Athletic. Tall. Nine years younger than Nate, and not clumsy in the least.

Nate could only imagine how much he paled in comparison.

If Amanda was looking at him in a romantic light. Which she wasn't. And, as he'd just been telling himself, he didn't want her to.

So this whole macho, territorial train of thought he had going on right now was ridiculous. "Have you met Amanda Kobayashi? She's Irene's goddaughter, and she's going to be the maid of honor at the wedding."

"Oh, hey, nice to meet you!" Brett lit up at the mention of the wedding. "I've been working hard to get the restaurant back up and running so they can have their reception there. We're aiming to have the grand reopening about two weeks before the ceremony."

"Awesome," Amanda said. "I heard you have great seafood."

Brett's chest puffed out. "Best on Cape Cod."

"I can't wait to try it."

"We've got a tasting set up in a couple of weeks. I'll make sure Irene and Bill invite you along."

"Ooh." Amanda rubbed her hands together. "I'm excited."

"Gotta jet, peeps—the boys are starving. But Chloe wanted you to call her, Nate. She's not sure if you need her to play the piano at the nursing home this weekend or not."

"I'll call her," Nate confirmed.

"Good deal." Brett slapped him on the back. "Have a nice night."

Amanda shot Nate a concerned look. "What's going on at the nursing home?"

"Nothing bad," he assured her. "We do a little mini service there on Saturday mornings. A lot of the residents aren't very mobile, so they appreciate the fact that we come to them."

"That's nice. You play hymns and stuff, too?"

He nodded. "I started out as a worship leader, so I'm all about the music."

Amanda knitted her eyebrows. "What's a worship leader?"

"Sorry, I forget that not everyone knows all the church terminology. For my first job, I was basically the music director at a big church out in Texas."

Her brow furrowed further. "You can't dance but they put you in charge of the music?"

He laughed. "Just because I can't dance, doesn't mean I can't play."

"What instrument do you play?"

"Piano, guitar, drums. Mostly guitar these days, but whatever's needed."

"Pierce played the piano," she said, her tone wistful.

"Did he play for a living?"

She shook her head. "No, he was a dentist. He played for fun."

"What type of music did he like?"

"Classical. Contemporary. Jazz. Anything, really. He liked learning new pieces. It was stress relief for him, I think."

"I can see that. Losing yourself in the music can be therapeutic."

"Exactly." She smiled. "Thanks for letting me talk about him. Most people get weird about it. Like they're worried any mention of him is going to make me bawl my eyes out."

"Even your in-laws?"

"Oh." She stiffened. "No. My mother-in-law doesn't speak

much English, though, so we'd need my sister-in-law to translate and…" She looked away. "We had a falling-out."

"I'm sorry to hear that," he said. "You can talk to me about him anytime."

After all, he'd been trained to be a good listener.

His offer had nothing—absolutely nothing—to do with the gratitude and appreciation gleaming in her clear blue eyes.

Chapter Four

Although Amanda had been skeptical about Hayden's baby-sitting abilities at first, he quickly proved that he was more than up for the job.

On Friday, he watched Ivy at Irene's apartment from four until seven, playing games, drawing pictures and even cooking her chicken nuggets for dinner. On Saturday, he took care of her all day while Irene walked Amanda through the ins and outs of the Candy Shack's point-of-sale and inventory control systems. According to Bill, who had supervised a trip to the playground, Hayden had spent two hours pushing Ivy on the swings, chasing Ivy down the slide and playing "tea party" with her and some imaginary friends in a clearing beneath the trees.

"Honey, you did such a good job with her today," Amanda said, handing over his hard-earned cash. "I'm impressed."

The boy blushed. "It was fun."

"Haybee is my bestest friend eber, eber, eber!" Ivy called out, doing a twirl. Her long brown hair was a rumpled mess, and it looked as though she'd torn her purple tutu, but she was happy, and Bill and Hayden were both still standing, so Amanda considered it a win.

"Do you want to babysit again next week?"

He turned to Bill. "Can I, Grandpa? It'll only take five

or six more weeks to save up enough money for the plane tickets."

Bill stroked his mustache. "Fine with me."

Glad to have at least a few hours of babysitting in place for the upcoming week, Amanda shuttled Ivy back home.

Although they'd been here for a few weeks already, their gorgeous, beachfront house still took Amanda's breath away. A two-story, ranch-style home set behind the dunes, it had been completely renovated by the previous owners, and the second floor boasted nearly panoramic views of Nantucket Sound.

Back when Pierce had purchased his life-insurance policy, Amanda had thought he was out of his mind. To her, it had seemed as though they were flushing hundreds of dollars down the drain each month. He'd always said, though, that his father's death had proved it was necessary, and now, as a result, Amanda owned this beautiful home free and clear. Unless something truly catastrophic happened, she'd never have to worry about money again.

She'd felt guilty about that at first, but she knew that Pierce had wanted her to have financial security. That he'd want her to make the best of a bad situation and live her best life now.

I miss you, Pierce. I'll always miss you.

Shortly after she got Ivy into her pajamas and then into bed, the doorbell rang. She ran quickly to the door in her bare feet, hoping that whoever was outside would refrain from setting the chimes off a second time. When Ivy was first falling asleep, any little noise could wake her.

She flung the door open, and a portly middle-aged man took a quick step back. "Amanda Kobayashi?"

"Yes. Hello."

"Oh, hi." He cleared his throat. "Sorry. I was expecting…"

This had happened enough times that Amanda could fill in the blanks. The worst was when it had happened at the airport, when she and Ivy were traveling to California after the funeral. She was grateful, of course, that the TSA agents took child kidnapping seriously, but it hurt when she had to prove to people, over and over, that she was Ivy's biological mom.

She arched an eyebrow at the man on her doorstep. "And you are…?"

"Right. Sorry. Here." He thrust a bouquet of flowers and a stuffed teddy bear at her. "I'm Rich Weatherbee, Joan's son. We all feel just terrible about what happened with your daughter."

Amanda peeked around him to look in the direction of Joan's house, which was just next door. "Is she out of the hospital?"

"She was only there for a couple of days, then my wife and I brought her up to Boston to stay with us for a while. Her nerves are shot."

Amanda bit her lip. "I'm sorry to hear that. She knows Ivy's okay, right?"

"She heard, but she's still very embarrassed and upset. She's been lonely and a little depressed since my dad died, but we never imagined…" He cleared his throat again. "I'm just so sorry for everything. If you need help with the medical expenses—"

"It's okay, Rich. We have good insurance."

"And you're not…" He pulled at his collar, looking pained. "You're not planning on suing?"

Amanda let out a little laugh. She was the last person who'd ever take someone to court…except maybe Caroline.

She'd wanted to take Caroline to court.

In those first few months after Pierce drowned, the burning-hot fury she'd felt toward her sister-in-law had been the only thing powerful enough to cut through the fog of her pain and grief.

But her father had told her that, despite Caroline's sibling relationship to Pierce, under the law, she'd had no duty to rescue him that day.

No duty to even try.

It still didn't make sense to Amanda. Even if her former best friend had had no legal obligation to help her brother, what about her moral responsibility? How could she have just stood there while he sank into the ocean, watching? How could she live with herself now?

If Amanda let herself dwell on those questions, the anger would consume her all over again, so she pulled herself back into the present moment, addressing the man on her porch. "It was an accident. Ivy's fine. I'm not going to ask Joan to babysit again, but I don't have any hard feelings."

"Would you, ah, maybe be willing to stop by sometime and tell her that?"

Amanda's forehead wrinkled. She held no hard feelings, but she also didn't think the job of making Joan feel better belonged to her.

Rich must have seen the reluctance on her face, because he rushed on. "She's been talking about selling her house and moving into a retirement home. I know she doesn't want to, but she's ashamed of herself for falling asleep like that and she's afraid that you're going to make her life miserable if she stays."

A flash of defensiveness sparked in Amanda's chest. Joan wasn't the victim in this whole scenario, and Amanda didn't like being cast in the role of villain. "I'd never make anyone's life miserable. That's not who I am."

"Of course not. It's just—" he tugged at his collar again "—she's been isolating herself since my dad died. She was so excited when you and your daughter moved in next door, and now…"

A bolt of inspiration struck her. "Hang on a second. Let me grab something from my purse." She ran to the kitchen and fished Nate's business card out of her wallet, then dashed back to the front hall. Holding it out to Rich, she said, "Here. This might help."

He squinted at the card. "Wise Widowhood?"

"It's a support group. At the church. A friend of mine facilitates it. Maybe you know him—Nate Anderson?"

"Oh, the pastor," Rich said, hitching up his pants. "Good guy. His services are always entertaining."

Entertainment wasn't the first thing that came to mind when Amanda thought about religion, but it didn't surprise her that people liked what Nate had to say. She'd certainly had a great time talking to him the other night.

She nodded at the card in Rich's hand. "Do you think she'd want to go to the group?"

"Are you going?"

She hadn't been planning on it, but maybe someone there—someone who'd been in her shoes—could help her figure out how to rid herself of the tight ball of anger she'd been carrying around since Pierce died.

Plus, she'd get to do something nice for her neighbor, so it was a win-win. "Sure, I'll go."

The fact that she'd get to see Nate two days before their next dance lesson had nothing to do with it. Nothing at all.

As usual, Sarah Jenkins was the first person to show up to the support-group meeting. She'd lost her husband two years ago, and although he'd had a long, slow decline thanks to Parkinson's disease, she was still reeling.

"How are you tonight, Sarah?" Nate asked, setting up the

chairs. This group wasn't big enough for the church hall, so they held their meetings in the conference room next to his office. It was large enough that they could create a circle of chairs away from the conference table, which lent the meeting a more relaxed, intimate feel.

"Oh, you know," Sarah said, laying out the snacks she'd brought on the table. A transplant from Great Britain, Sarah held fast to the customs and cuisine of her youth. Right now, she was arranging platters of cucumber sandwiches, deviled eggs and sausage rolls. Nate's stomach rumbled. He never ate dinner before this meeting when Sarah was on snack duty.

"A little birdie told me you were in the dance studio last Thursday," she added, her eyes twinkling. "Taken up a new hobby, have you?"

He sighed and gave her a good-natured eye roll. "Irene wants me to dance at her wedding."

Sarah laughed. "Has she never seen you on the dance floor?"

"She has. Hence the lessons."

"Well," Sarah said, biting back a smile, "that little birdie also told me you went out to dinner with your dance partner afterward."

Nate shook his head, amused. Did everyone in this town always have to know *everything*? "We grabbed a couple of slices at Franco's. The height of romance."

"Who is she?"

"Irene hasn't told you?"

"I haven't seen Irene all week."

"Amanda's her goddaughter. She's going to be the maid of honor at the wedding."

Sarah grinned. "Oh, that's right! The young widow! That's perfect!"

Nate scrunched his brow. "It's perfect that she's a widow?"

"No, no." Sarah laughed that off. "Of course not. But it might make her perfect for *you*."

Nate sighed. He loved and appreciated his entire congregation, but the ladies in this support group always seemed a little too invested in his life. Specifically, his romantic life. Or lack thereof.

"Sarah. We're not dating. She's not perfect for me. She's way too young."

"Don't be daft. You're both adults, aren't you?"

"Yes, but—" He caught himself before he told her about the Harvard PhD program, because this wasn't how he wanted to break the news that he was leaving to the congregants of his church. "She's young, that's all I'm saying. Very young."

"I was eighteen when I met my Alfred," Sarah said, a starry-eyed expression on her face, "and we were married for fifty-two years."

"And Danielle was eighteen when she met me." He wasn't sure why he threw that little tidbit into the mix, but there it was. If he started dating another much younger woman, he knew it would upset his mother-in-law.

Which, if he was interested in Amanda, he could live with, but it could make things awkward for Hayden, and he didn't want to force his son to deal with Cheryl's displeasure.

"Oh, Nate." Sarah's eyes went watery at the mention of his late wife. "Such a tragedy."

"Yes," he said simply, because sometimes the newer widows—he was currently the only widower in the group—wanted to dwell on each other's heartbreak in a way that wasn't healthy.

"Excuse me, Nate?" Joan Weatherbee, a petite older woman who liked to dress as though she lived in Florida year-round, peeked her head into the conference room. "Is this the Wise Widowhood meeting?"

"This is it, Joan." Nate was genuinely happy to see her. She'd disappeared after Ivy's accident, and he'd been worried about her. "Come on in."

She took a tentative step into the room, her colorful floral-print shirt matching her bright pink lipstick. "Is this... everyone?"

The Wise Widows were a small but committed bunch. "We'll probably have a few more trickle in over the next few minutes."

"Is Amanda Kobayashi coming?"

Nate frowned. "I don't think so."

"Oh." Joan held herself stiff, and Nate couldn't tell whether she was disappointed or relieved.

"Did she tell you she'd be here?" The hopeful lift in his chest concerned him. *You're moving away at the end of the summer. Don't get attached.*

"Not me," Joan said. "My son."

He shook his head. "I don't know, Joan. She's never been here before."

Her shoulders sagged. "I hoped I'd have a chance to talk to her."

"Deviled egg?" Sarah asked sweetly, offering the plate to Joan.

The two ladies got to chatting, and Nate finished setting up the chairs. A handful of other women arrived, and Nate opened the meeting with a prayer. They went around the circle and introduced themselves briefly. Then they opened their workbooks and took turns reading paragraphs from today's lesson.

Partway through the passage, a jolt of awareness hit Nate, and he looked up. Amanda was frozen in the doorway, her blond hair falling around her shoulders like sunbeams, uncertainty splashed across her face.

He gave her a small smile and a discreet wave. *Come on in.*

She tiptoed into the corner and leaned against the wall. A couple of the women in the circle glanced at her, then focused their attention back on the passage being read. Nate tried to follow suit but found himself sneaking glance after glance at Amanda.

Her blond hair.

Her blue eyes.

The elegant curve of her neck.

The way her earrings sparkled in the light.

He forced himself to look away. This was not good. He was acting like a teenage boy with a crush, and he needed to nip it in the bud. Fast.

When they reached the next paragraph break, Nate interrupted the reading. "Ladies, before we continue with the discussion, we have another visitor tonight. Amanda—" he beckoned her over with a welcoming gesture "—come and join us."

"Hi," she said to the group, sliding into a chair while simultaneously chewing her lip. "Sorry to interrupt."

"Since Amanda missed the introductions and it's her first meeting, let's do them again. I'm Nate, and I lost my wife, Danielle, twelve years ago."

They went around the circle again until they hit Joan, who was pulling so hard at her chunky coral necklace that Nate thought it might break. "I'm Joan and my husband passed away seven months ago, but that's not actually why I'm here tonight." She turned to Amanda, her knuckles white around her necklace, which she had clutched to her chest. "I'm so sorry. I didn't mean to put your baby in danger. If someone had hurt my son the way I hurt Ivy—" her chin wobbled and the first sob burst forth "—I don't know what I would have done."

Sarah, who was sitting next to Joan, made a sympathetic sound in the back of her throat and grabbed a box of tissues.

"You didn't hurt Ivy, Joan," Amanda said softly. "It was an accident. She snuck out."

"While I was sleeping!" Joan wailed. "She could have drowned!"

"But she didn't," Amanda said firmly, and the attraction Nate had been trying to dampen flared into something bigger, something brighter. Respect.

And not simply the common courtesy and respect that he automatically afforded to everyone, but an appreciation that was deeper and harder-earned.

She wasn't simply a pretty face or a graceful dancer or an intriguing dinner companion. She was compassionate. And compassion was a trait that went a long, long way with Nate.

"I could have killed her!"

Amanda shot a glance at Nate. "Is there somewhere Joan and I can go that's more private?"

"My office," he said, rising quickly from his seat. "Sarah, you're in charge for the next few minutes. You know the drill. Finish the reading and then set the timer for three-minute shares."

He helped Joan, who was still clutching her necklace and sobbing, to her feet, then led her and Amanda from the conference room to his office.

Joan sat and tried to catch her breath. He caught Amanda's eye, pointed to himself and mouthed, *Stay? Or go?*

Stay, she mouthed back. *Please.*

Satisfaction rippled through him. He was always happy when he had a chance to be of service to others, but to be of service to *her* added a whole other level of fulfillment to the task at hand.

But he wasn't going to think about why that was just now.

"I'm sorry," Joan choked out again. "So very, very sorry."

"Honestly, Joan—" Amanda put her hand on the older lady's forearm "—I know you lost your husband recently. I know what that's like. I was in such a fog for a while that I don't even remember telling my parents that I wanted to go ahead and sell my house!"

Joan sniffled. "You sold your house?"

"My house in Boston, yes. My parents put the real estate agent's contract in front of me and I signed it without stopping to think about it. At the time, I just didn't care."

Joan took her hand off her necklace and raised it to her mouth. "Oh, my."

Nate was impressed by how effectively Amanda had managed to reroute the conversation. He was also grateful that she'd invited him to be a fly on the wall—he was interested to hear what she had to say about her move.

"Then we got a good offer, and my mom told me I should take it, that I could stay with them for as long as I wanted, that she'd help me take care of Ivy and get her into a good preschool. I needed help at that point, so I figured, why not?"

"Where do your parents live?" Joan asked.

"California."

Joan's eyes rounded. "So far away."

"That was by design. After Pierce died, I needed them, but they reminded me quick enough why I'd moved to Massachusetts in the first place."

"Why?" Joan asked. Given their conversation at the pizza parlor, Nate was pretty sure he knew why, but when Amanda answered, he was surprised.

"Well, my mom signed Ivy up for a beauty pageant, so there was that."

"A beauty pageant?" Nate repeated incredulously. "She's so little."

"Oh, you can put babies in beauty pageants," Amanda said, lifting an eyebrow at him. "Ask me how I know."

"Good grief." Concern had edged out the shame and sadness in Joan's eyes. "I hope you put your foot down and said no."

Amanda smiled, but it was tight and small. "I did more than say no. I moved right out of their house, stayed with one of my brothers for a few weeks and bought my house here on the Cape sight unseen."

Joan's jaw dropped, and the same level of shock streaked through Nate. Amanda was a strong woman. You had to be strong to pick up the pieces after losing your spouse, but she was next level. "How did you know you'd like it?" Joan asked.

"I saw pictures online. Plus, Irene toured it for me."

"And you know Irene from…?"

"She's my godmother, but really, she's more like a second mom. When I came to Massachusetts for college, Irene was the one who helped me move into my dorm. She'd drive up to Amherst and bring me to Cape Cod for all the minor holidays, even though it was a three-hour drive each way. She sent me care packages and let me move into her apartment two summers in a row when I got a job as a lifeguard down here, and she didn't charge me a dime of rent. She's a little brisk on the outside, but—Nate can attest to this—she has a heart of gold."

"She does," he agreed. "My dad's never been happier."

"Why didn't you move back to Boston?" Joan asked. "You must have friends there."

Amanda looked away. "I used to have friends there. After Pierce died, I...let most of those friendships die, too."

"Oh, honey." Joan leaned in and patted Amanda on the hand. "I'm sure you could pick them right back up where you left off."

"Not all of them." Pain—and a hint of anger—flashed across her face. "Plus, I didn't have a job waiting for me in Boston."

Joan's face fell. "Have you been able to get back to work since the—" her voice quavered "—the incident?"

Amanda smiled. "Actually, yes. Just part-time for now, but Nate's son, Hayden, has been babysitting Ivy after school, and he's been fantastic."

Joan turned to Nate. "Oh, Hayden. Such a good boy."

Nate stuck his hands in his pockets. "That he is."

"And you're a good dad."

He shrugged. "I do my best."

"You do," Joan said. "With everything. We're so fortunate to have you here at the church. Our very own good shepherd."

Nate rubbed the back of his neck. He was glad to be of service to his congregation, but he worried about how they were going to react to his decision to leave.

Each pastor brought his own skills and talents to the job. Would whomever Wychmere Community Church hired next keep Nate's music ministry intact? Would they find someone to take over for him on the guitar?

And what about the Wise Widows? There had been no support group for grief when Nate joined WCC—it had been one of his passion projects. If the new pastor wasn't widowed, would he be able to gain the members' trust and guide each of them through their own unique grief journey? Would he want to dedicate time to it, or would he simply shut it down?

Should Nate give his notice now? Or wait? His father-in-law, Tim, had said giving thirty days' notice was more than sufficient, but Nate had been praying about it, and he thought he should probably start the ball rolling on finding his successor sooner rather than later.

His in-laws were planning to come to town for his dad's wedding, though, so he was going to hold off on making any firm decisions until then.

"You okay now, Joan?" he asked. "Should we get back to the meeting?"

"Oh, yes." She looked back and forth between him and Amanda. "Sorry for distracting you both."

"I'm sure I'm speaking for everyone in that room when I say that I'm really glad you came out tonight. I hope you'll come back again next week."

"I might," she said, looking brighter than he'd seen her since her husband passed away. "I just might."

But how many more weeks would the group itself be there? Nate simply wasn't sure.

Chapter Five

When Amanda got to the dance studio on Thursday evening, Nate was already there. He'd worn running shoes this time, plus black track pants—the kind with white stripes up the sides—and a T-shirt.

"You know we're not going to be dancing in gym clothes at the wedding, right?" She bit back a smile as she greeted him.

"There's a method to my madness. Start comfy, then work my way up to the suit and tie over the next few weeks."

She grinned. "Smart."

"You look nice."

She'd taken the opposite tack from him and worn a skirt and heels tonight. She was five-eight, so she usually opted for flats to avoid feeling like a giant, but Nate was tall enough that the extra two inches wouldn't matter. "Thanks."

The dance instructor quickly reviewed the basic box step with them—slow, quick, quick, slow, quick, quick—then reminded Nate where to put his hands. They faced each other, and he placed his left hand on her right shoulder, then lightly clasped her hand.

"You're doing great," Amanda said, hoping to reassure him so he stopped standing so stiffly, and he gave her hand a grateful squeeze.

Ellen turned on the music and started counting the beat. Nate swallowed. "Watch your feet."

On one, he stepped forward and she stepped back, but on two, he stepped to the wrong side.

"Right forward, left side, right closed, Nate," the instructor said.

"Yes, got it."

Ellen restarted the music and counted them in again. This time, they made it through the first three steps, but he got tripped up when he had to step back.

Ellen huffed and restarted the music again.

Nate winced. "Sorry."

Amanda smiled to put him at ease. "It's fine."

After a few more false starts, Ellen stopped the music and put her hands on her hips. "Let's take a five-minute break."

Then she marched outside, leaving Amanda flabbergasted by her impatience. "What's up with her?"

Nate gave Amanda a rueful smile. "I heard she had an offer on the studio lined up, but it just fell through. Plus, she doesn't normally teach adults, and I'm terrible at this."

Amanda chewed her lip. "If she doesn't normally teach adults, then how…?"

"Irene called in a favor."

"Oh, of course." She took a closer look around the studio. The unicorn mural on the side wall probably should have been a clue. It was so cute in here—it would be a great place for classes like Zumba and kickboxing.

She wondered if it had an office or a storage room in the back. The big gym nearby didn't have childcare, and it would be nice to have some exercise classes that moms like her could attend without having to book a babysitter.

Too bad Ellen was selling. Otherwise, she might have suggested the other woman look into what adding adult classes and childcare might entail.

"Ivy would like it here," she said.

"You should bring her. Without me. I'm hopeless."

"Take it easy on my friend Nate, will you?" she teased. "He's new at this."

The tension in his shoulders eased a little at her joke. "I don't want to step on you."

"I've got an idea." She kicked off her heels. "Maybe *I* should step on you. Break the ice."

He laughed. "What?"

She darted forward and stepped on his toe really quick. "There. See?"

He gaped at her. "You stepped on me."

"And it didn't hurt, did it? See? You try it."

The disbelief on his face slid into bemusement. "Uh, pass. I'm a lot heavier than you are."

She stepped on him again, but instead of darting away immediately, she wobbled, and he put his hands on her waist to steady her. A little zip of...*something* raced through her at his touch.

She tried to ignore it. Pierce had only been gone for a year and a half—it was way too soon. If she stuck to the decision she'd made right after he died, she wouldn't date again for at least fifteen years.

Backing away, she said, "Take off your shoes. Try it."

"Nope." He pushed his glasses higher up his nose. "Not purposely stepping on you."

"Well, take off your shoes, anyway. That way if you do step on me, it won't hurt."

Chuckling, he shook his head. "You're something else."

"Loosen up and lose the shoes, Mr. Anderson. You don't have to impress anybody here."

"You really want me to take off my shoes. Right now."

She waggled her bare toes at him. "Yes."

"All right," he conceded, then sat in one of the folding

chairs in the corner so he could untie his laces and set his shoes neatly against the wall.

"Great!" She liked it that he trusted her enough to follow her suggestion. "Now, maybe starting with the box step isn't the best idea. Maybe we should start by swaying."

He gave her a quizzical look as he rose from the chair.

"Here," she said, resting her left hand on top of his right shoulder and reaching for his other hand. "Same hand positions."

He placed his right hand on her back, and that frisson of whatever it was came rushing back in.

It's too soon, she reminded herself again. She still loved Pierce, and she wanted to be loyal to him. Any zing she felt around Nate was most likely due to the fact that she hadn't stood this close to a man—hadn't held a man's hand or smelled the fresh, citrusy scent of his aftershave—in such a long time.

She cleared her throat. "Now, we're just going to sway side to side. Don't move your feet—just transfer your weight from one foot to the other."

He did it, and she matched her movement to his. "Perfect. See? You can dance just fine."

He snorted, his eyes on his feet, but he kept swaying.

"Look at me, Nate. Not your feet."

"If I don't look, I won't see where I'm going."

"You don't need to see. We're hardly moving."

He looked up, his eyes overflowing with worry, and without thinking about it, she took her hand off his shoulder and smoothed her fingers over the furrow between his brows. "Relax. I don't care if you trip up or make a mistake."

The worry in his eyes melted into gratitude. Good. His son had saved Ivy's life—Nate really didn't need to fret about anything around her. She was always going to be on his side.

She placed her hand back on his shoulder. "Now, really

slowly, we're going to turn in a circle. Just rotate your feet a little bit every time you move."

They started turning. "Hey, I'm dancing!" Nate said.

Amanda smiled. "You are."

"This isn't so hard."

"Once you get the hang of it, it's not bad at all."

"So we can credit your mad dance skills to cotillion, huh?"

Laughing, she stepped on his foot again.

"What about the beauty pageants? Did you have to dance for those?"

"Ugh." She pulled a face. "No, but I did have to display a talent. Some girls dance, but you can sing or play an instrument or do gymnastics or recite a monologue—whatever you want, really."

"What did you do?"

"When I was little, I sang. When I got older, martial arts."

His eyebrows shot up. "Really?"

She smirked. "Five older brothers, Pastor. They made sure I knew how to defend myself."

"What kind of martial arts?"

"When I was young, I did tae kwon do, so that's what I'd do for the talent shows." She grinned. "My mom *hated* it." Her brothers had loved it, though, and although they'd never come to her shows before, they'd all started showing up for her martial-arts demos. Her popularity with the other contestants had shot through the roof, and she'd actually walked away from the pageant circuit with a bunch of good friends.

Once she'd moved to Massachusetts for college, she'd lost touch with most of them, which had been okay with her at the time, since she'd had Caroline. Now, of course, it was easy to wish she'd never met her former best friend, although it was a weird catch-22, since without Caroline, she'd never have met Pierce.

"Have you kept it up? The tae kwon do?"

She shook her head. "I switched to kickboxing in college. You can do classes right at the gym."

"Wow. You're full of surprises."

"What about you?"

"Do I kickbox or do tae kwon do? No."

"But you obviously do something to stay in shape."

His lips curved up. "Do I, now?"

Her cheeks heated. "I mean, you do, don't you?" Clearly, he was no bodybuilder, but he was trim. No dad bod or middle-aged spread in sight.

"Hayden and I walk a lot with the dog. And I swim."

"In the ocean?"

He nodded. "In the summer, yeah. The rest of the year, I try to hit the pool at the YMCA two or three times a week."

"You check for riptides before you go out, right?"

"Of course."

Inwardly, she gave a little sigh of relief. She still loved the ocean, but she wasn't naive to its dangers anymore. "Ever seen a shark?"

"At the Y? No."

She stepped on his foot again. "Stop teasing me."

He laughed, and she stepped back into their sway. "Never seen a shark in the ocean, either."

"Whales? Seals? Sea otters?"

"I've seen seals and sea otters while I'm swimming, but not up close and personal. Jellyfish, though," he said, wincing, "you have to watch out for those."

"Do you scuba dive?"

"No."

"Snorkel?"

"I've tried it, but the water here's pretty murky."

"True." She and Pierce had gone to Hawaii for their honeymoon. The snorkeling there had been out of this world.

But thinking about her honeymoon, about how much hope she'd had back then, would only make her sad, so she changed the subject. "What kind of dog do you have?"

"Lucy's a cocker spaniel."

"Aww, cute."

"She's a good girl."

"What color?"

"White with brown spots."

"How old is she?"

"Three."

"So just a little bit older than Ivy. Was getting a dog your idea? Or Hayden's?"

"My dad's, actually."

She grinned. "No way. Good for Bill. Is he taking her with him after the wedding?"

"Ha!" Nate's hand flexed on her shoulder blade. "I'd like to see him try taking that dog away from Hayden."

She smiled. Hayden was a good kid. Ivy talked about him nonstop.

"He was out walking Lucy the night he found Ivy on the jetty."

"Aww, I owe her a treat, then." She owed all of the Andersons more than she could ever repay.

If Caroline had demonstrated even half the initiative that Hayden had shown the night he found Ivy, Pierce might still be alive. Ivy might still have her father. And Amanda might not be a widow, enjoying the company of another man.

The thought seared like acid, and she stumbled, her mother-in-law's face flashing through her mind. *Miyoko would be so disappointed in you.*

Nate stopped dancing. "What happened? Did I trip you?"

"No, I—" She glanced around the studio. Where was Ellen? Why hadn't she come back? "I need some air."

Without even bothering to slip her shoes back on, she pushed her way out the front door onto Main Street, letting the nighttime breeze cool the sting of her guilt.

Nate frowned at Irene. "What do you mean, she's not coming?" He was standing at the counter of the Candy Shack, with block after block of fudge on display in the case in front of him. Orange cranberry, key lime pie and strawberry shortcake were just a few of the flavors currently calling his name.

A week had passed since his last dance lesson with Amanda, and he'd been looking forward to tonight ever since.

He'd hoped to see her before tonight, actually, but she hadn't come to the Wise Widowhood meeting the other day, and every time he'd picked up Hayden from babysitting, he'd discovered that Amanda had swung by early to collect Ivy and was no longer there.

Irene shrugged. "Said she has a headache."

Nate frowned harder. "Did I do something to offend her?"

Irene gave him a sharp look. "*Did* you?"

He wracked his brain. "I don't think so." But she'd certainly left the dance studio in a hurry last Thursday. And he still had no idea why. "We were talking about Lucy, and then all of a sudden she just bolted. Didn't even stop to put on her shoes."

"Why wasn't she wearing shoes?"

His lips curved up. "She was stepping on my feet so I wouldn't feel bad if I accidentally stepped on hers."

Irene laughed and shook her head. "That girl."

"She's something else." So pretty and polished on the outside, but when you scratched the surface, she was surprisingly funny and fierce. He could totally see her practicing tae kwon do with her five older brothers...or kicking the stuffing out of a punching bag at the gym.

It was charming. And disarming.

And he wanted to learn about all the little things that made her tick.

"I was going to drop off dinner for her and Ivy after the store closes," Irene said. "Already placed a take-out order for fish and chips at the Barnacle Bakery. But since you're here, why don't you grab Hayden from upstairs and the two of you can run it over? I have a few things to do after I close."

Nate smirked. "Like what?"

"Like inventory, young man," Irene retorted, hands on her hips.

He lifted his eyebrows. "Mmm-hmm."

"This is a very busy store."

"I know it is," he said evenly.

"We go through our candy quickly."

"I know you do."

"Then what's the problem? Surely you wouldn't want to add extra errands to an old lady's already overflowing plate."

He snorted. She was as spry and energetic as women half her age. "Irene, you only play the old-lady card when you want something."

Her eyes flared with indignation. "I do want something. For you to take dinner over to Amanda."

"Why?"

"I just told you why! I'm busy!"

"You love being busy." In fact, she loved it so much that Nate couldn't picture her actually handing Amanda the reins to the candy store and retiring.

She threw her hands in the air. "Did it ever occur to you that maybe I want a little extra time with your father?"

"And did it ever occur to *you* that Amanda and I are onto

your not-so-subtle matchmaking scheme? It's not going to work. We've talked about it, and we're not interested in each other like that."

Irene scoffed.

"We're not. I'm too old for her and she's too—" he struggled to think of the right word for her "—*everything* for me."

Irene laughed. "Not interested, my foot. You should see your face right now. You're besotted."

He schooled his features into a blank look. "I'm *not* besotted."

"Oh, young man." She gave his arm an amused little pat. "You keep telling yourself that."

The bell over the door dinged, and Hayden trooped inside, followed by Nate's dad. "I'm not babysitting tonight, Dad. Ms. Kobayashi's sick. Grandpa and Miss Perkins ordered—"

"Irene, Hayden. Call me Irene," the woman in question interrupted.

Hayden flushed. "Irene, right. Sorry. Anyway, they ordered dinner for Ms. K and Ivy. Grandpa said we can bring it over to them."

Nate rubbed his forehead. He was smart enough to know when he'd been outmaneuvered. Dramatically clutching his heart, he looked at his dad and faked a stumble. "*Et tu*, Father?"

His dad grinned.

Hayden looked back and forth between them, confused. "It's *y tu*, not *et tu* in Spanish, Dad." Apparently, Shakespeare's *Julius Caesar* wasn't on the curriculum for the sixth grade.

"Thanks, champ."

"And if you're trying to speak French, your accent's terrible."

"It's a Latin phrase, kiddo."

Hayden scrunched his nose. "Why are you speaking Latin to Grandpa?"

"Doesn't matter." He threw an arm around his son's shoulders. It wouldn't be long until Hayden was as tall as he was. If Nate had to guess, he'd say his son was already five-four or five-five. His whole childhood was passing so quickly. He was already in middle school, and in just six more years, he'd finish high school and then be on his way to college. They needed to make the most of the time they had now. "Should we go pick up the food?"

"Can we get takeout, too?"

Although Nate wasn't the world's best cook, he and Hayden rarely indulged in fast food. It was expensive, for one thing, and generally much less healthy than what they could make at home. Sometimes, though, a boy and his dad needed to bond. And how better to do it than over a nice, greasy order of fish and chips, extra tartar sauce included? "Sure, why not?"

Nate called the restaurant and placed their order, and then the two of them walked over to retrieve it. It was nice out, and the days were getting noticeably longer. At the beginning of March, the sun had been setting around five thirty, but now it was staying light until almost eight o'clock.

"Bummer I didn't get to babysit today," Hayden commented.

"Really? I thought you might enjoy having the night off."

Hayden shrugged. "Ivy's cute. It's easy money."

"I'm glad you're having fun with it."

They picked up four huge orders of fish and chips—two for them, and two for Amanda and Ivy—and took it all back to the car, which was parked in front of the Candy Shack. Once they were inside, the warm, rich smell of the batter-fried cod hit him hard, and Nate's mouth watered. He hadn't had fish and chips in a while, but it had always been one of his favorite restaurant meals.

They drove to Amanda's house quickly, Hayden sneaking fries whenever he thought Nate was preoccupied by the road.

"Got any homework tonight?" Nate asked.

"Nope. Finished it at school."

"How's Spanish class going, anyway?"

Hayden gave him a thumbs-up. *"Bueno."*

"Your test today went well?"

"Sí, papa."

"That'll be a good skill to have if you keep it up." Nate could speak only the most rudimentary Spanish; he should've taken the opportunity to learn more when he'd lived in Texas. Dani had been fluent, though, so he'd deferred to her whenever they'd been in a situation where Spanish had been required. "Your mom could speak flawless Spanish. Grandpa Tim can, too."

"I know, Dad. Don't worry. I'll take it again next year."

Nate nodded as he pulled into Amanda's driveway. "Good man."

They rang the bell, Nate holding the take-out bag with the fish and chips.

Amanda opened the door, her eyes wide with surprise at the sight of them, but Ivy, who was standing right beside her, was the very picture of joy.

"Haybee!" she screamed, like a teenage girl at a Taylor Swift concert. She leaped forward and latched onto his left leg. "It you! It really you! At my house!"

Hayden patted her hair. "Hey, silly."

"Come see my room," she ordered.

"Umm—" Hayden looked to Amanda for direction.

"Now, Mama. He see my room now!"

Amanda sighed and stepped back from the door, opening it wider. "Come on in."

Ivy squealed again, let go of Hayden's leg and tugged on his hand, all while chanting his name. "Haybee, Haybee, Haybee, we go see my room."

Nate held up the take-out bag. "We didn't mean to intrude. We heard you were under the weather, so we brought dinner."

Amanda gave him a stiff smile and fluttered her hands. "It's fine. You made Ivy's day. Come in." She led him into the kitchen while Ivy dragged Hayden upstairs.

The house was gorgeous. Open plan with golden hardwood flooring that ran through the living room and into the kitchen, which had hardwood cabinets, steel appliances and white countertops. The walls were painted a pale peach, the windows overlooking the beach were both tall and wide and there were two skylights that undoubtedly sent sunlight streaming over the dining table during the day.

Nate could imagine Amanda sitting there in the morning, nursing a cup of coffee, the sun making her hair shine like gold. Danielle had been a brunette, but he remembered cozy mornings like that with her. He *missed* cozy mornings like that. He'd love to experience the easy comfort and happiness of those mornings again with someone like—

He slammed the door on that train of thought. He liked Amanda a lot, but she'd been clear about what she wanted from him, and cozy mornings together were not included in that plan.

Setting down the fish and chips on the counter, he said, "Nice place you've got here."

"Thanks."

"You feeling okay? Irene said you had a headache."

"I took one of my migraine pills. It doesn't take too long to kick in."

"Migraines, huh? I thought maybe you were avoiding me."

She winced and looked down, her cheeks flushing pink.

Oh. She was *avoiding you.*

His heart sank.

"It's not you," she protested. But in keeping with tonight's Shakespeare theme, he suspected that "the lady doth protest too much."

"Why'd you run out of the studio last week? I *did* hurt you, didn't I?"

"No, not at all."

"Are you sure? I shouldn't have taken off my shoes, should I? I knew that was a mistake." He'd gotten too comfortable around her, too familiar. He'd scared her off.

She shook her head. "I'm glad you took them off. It made you loosen up a little. You're so scared of making a mistake that you hold yourself way too stiff."

"Then what happened? I thought we were having a nice time."

She looked away again. "We were," she said. "Too nice."

For a second, he thought he'd misheard her. When he realized he hadn't, he froze.

"Sorry," she mumbled, the pink in her cheeks deepening to red. "I know you're not interested in me like that."

Half of him wanted to do a fist pump, but the other half knew he had to do the right thing. *Lord*, he prayed, *give me the right words*. "It's not that I'm *not* interested in you. But Hayden and I are moving in a few months, and you're vulnerable, and so much younger, and as a pastor, it wouldn't be right…"

"I know." The blush on her face was finally fading. "And I still love Pierce. I'm not ready to move on."

Nate nodded. He got that. He'd been in that same place for years and years and years. "You don't have to move on, Amanda. Not with me, not with anyone. Not until you're ready."

"My mother-in-law lost her husband sixteen years ago. She's never moved on."

"That's okay, too." Even the Apostle Paul, in 1 Corinthians 7, had said that widows could stay single or remarry, whichever made the most sense in a given situation. "You don't have to do anything you don't want to do. Ever."

"My mom thinks I should get back out there and start dating again."

He gave her a good-humored smile. "The same mom you moved three thousand miles to get away from? That mom?"

Huffing out a laugh, she said, "I mean, when you put it like that..."

He leaned his hip against the counter. "Should we cancel the rest of the dance lessons?"

She hesitated for only a split second before shaking her head. "No way, buddy. You need those lessons." Her eyes twinkled as she flashed him a playful, yet somehow still pitying smile.

And even though they'd mutually agreed—again—that it was better not to take things in a romantic direction, hearing her place him so clearly in the friend zone still stung.

"Well, *buddy*, I'll go grab Hayden and we'll get out of your hair."

"You guys should stay for dinner." She nodded at the fish and chips on the counter. "Ivy will be over the moon."

Her invitation soothed the sting, and he took four plates out of the kitchen cupboard while she went to round up the kids. As they ate and talked and laughed at the way Ivy chattered throughout the meal, showing off for Hayden, Nate imagined what it might be like to have dinner like this every night: a family of four instead of two families of two.

And as he did, he couldn't help but wonder if not pouncing on Amanda's expression of interest—conflicted though it may have been—had been a big mistake.

Chapter Six

Amanda sat in the pew next to Sarah, Joan and a few other Wise Widows and smoothed her skirt over her thighs. She'd seen Nate a bunch of times since their fish-and-chip dinner at her house two and a half weeks ago, but coming to see him here, in action as a pastor, felt different. Intentional in a way that going to the Wise Widowhood meetings and dance lessons did not.

Guilt slammed into her, and she tried to tamp it down. He was a friend. That's all. And friends supported friends.

Even if she thought Nate was drop-dead handsome, she'd been honest with him that she was still in love with Pierce, and he'd accepted it. End of discussion.

Except she still thought about him an awful lot...

Sarah, who'd powdered her nose and pulled her graying hair back into a Victorian-style bun for church, leaned closer and whispered, "Did you get Ivy settled in the childcare room?"

"Yes. Have you seen the dollhouse they have in there? She was thrilled!"

Sarah squeezed her forearm. "You should bring her back again next weekend. Give yourself a breather. Spend a little quiet time with the Lord."

Amanda gave her a weak smile. "We'll see."

Quiet time with the Lord sounded like her worst nightmare. To be honest, she'd rather face off with Him in a kick-boxing match.

No, Amanda wasn't here to spend time with God. She was here to see Nate play the guitar.

It was all the Wise Widows had been able to talk about before the meeting this past Tuesday. Apparently, Nate and Chloe Weston, Brett Richardson's sister, had played a new song at the nursing-home service last week, bringing some of the residents to tears, and they were debuting it at church today.

The little church was much smaller than the one Amanda had grown up attending in California, and smaller, too, than the church she and Pierce had belonged to in Boston. It was charming, though. White clapboard on the outside with dark wooden pews and stained-glass windows inside.

Cute, she'd say. Cozy. Quintessential Cape Cod.

Pierce would be upset if he knew she'd stopped attending services after his death. Whenever disappointments would hit, he'd say "God is good in the hard times, too," or "God has a plan."

Amanda didn't believe that anymore. Or, more accurately, she didn't want to believe it. Because what kind of plan included the untimely death of her spouse?

She thought back to the Bible passage the Wise Widows had discussed this past week: *Behold, happy is the man whom God correcteth: Therefore despise not thou the chastening of the Almighty: For he maketh sore, and bindeth up: he woundeth, and his hands make whole.*

Had God taken Pierce to teach her a lesson? If so, she had no clue what it was. And if she couldn't figure it out, did it mean He was going to keep throwing tragedies at her until she got it? What other mean tricks did God have up His sleeve?

In the year and half since Pierce had passed away, she'd gone around and around and around, trying to figure out why he'd done what he'd done that day, why God had let him do it, and it was exhausting. She was so tired of trying to figure it out. So tired of carrying that mental load.

She knew she could lay it at the feet of the Father, but she didn't want to. In all honesty, she'd rather be angry with God than angry with Pierce.

Sarah's sharp inhale snapped Amanda out of her thoughts, and she looked up to see a pretty blonde woman take a seat at the upright piano on the left side of the altar. Next to her, an older man got situated behind his drum set while Nate positioned himself between them holding his guitar.

Dressed in gray pants and a light blue, button-up shirt, he looked good up there. Warm. Authentic. More confident than she'd ever seen him before.

If he was even half this confident on the dance floor...

A tiny thrill shot through her at the thought.

Yikes, if she'd thought telling him that she wasn't ready to move on would curb her attraction to him, she'd been dead wrong.

Stop it. You're in church.

Guilt cinched itself around her chest and squeezed.

Nate spoke into the microphone. "Morning, everybody. Good turnout today."

A few soft chuckles sounded in the crowd.

"You all know how much I love church music. Music is about emotion, about feeling. It's a way for us to honor God, worship God, without words. It's a way for us to connect with each other, and connect with ourselves. It's about the heart, not the head, and we know from the Bible that the heart is where Christ lives inside each and every one of us."

He looked out over his congregation as he continued, "We're going to sing some new songs for you at the end of the service today, and I hope you'll stay for that. But right now, I'd like you all to stand and join us in singing one of the greatest hymns of all time, 'Amazing Grace.'"

Amanda and the Wise Widows stood along with the rest of the assembly, and as the band struck the first notes of the hymn, chills raced up and down Amanda's arms.

She'd sung this song at church with her grandparents when she was just a small child. She'd sung it at her grandmother's funeral, watching heartbreak crack her grandfather wide-open with each note he sang, and then she'd sung it at his funeral, too.

This song was love and comfort and sadness, all wrapped together.

It was the key to a thousand memories, a thousand moments lost but shared.

It spoke, as Nate had just said, directly to her heart.

Sarah handed her a tissue. "This song always gets to me, too," she said softly.

Startled, Amanda realized that tears were dripping down her face. She took the tissue and wiped them away, then took a deep breath, joining in for the third verse:

The Lord hath promised good to me,
His word my hope secures;
He will my shield and portion be
As long as life endures.

Her eyes watered and her chest ached. She wanted the kind of faith her grandparents had had, the same kind Pierce had had as well.

She was tired of trying to figure out what Pierce's death meant with her head—maybe it was time to stop trying to piece it all together and let God speak to her heart.

After all, it wasn't God who'd gone in the water that day. Pierce was the one who'd made that choice.

She didn't want to be angry with him—it made her feel disloyal—but he was gone. Her anger wouldn't hurt him. Her loyalty wouldn't serve him. And he'd never be able to comfort her over the fact that he wasn't here anymore.

God was still here, though, willing to shield and console her if she could put her anger aside and turn to Him.

I'm here, Lord. I'm listening.

There was no lightning and no thunderbolts, but something inside her eased just the smallest, most minuscule amount. The hymn ended and she sat, curious to hear what Nate would say next.

On Monday night, Nate met Amanda at the Candy Shack. They had a tasting to attend at the Sea Glass Inn.

His dad and Irene should have been with them, but Irene had come down with a bad cold over the weekend, and his dad had decided to stay in to cook her some soup. When Nate had suggested that they reschedule, Irene had proclaimed, "Nonsense! Your father and I trust you two to make good choices."

When he'd asked about how the babysitting would work, Irene had promised to stay quarantined in her room, away from the kids.

So here Nate was, opening his car door for Amanda, so they could run another wedding-related errand. This time, though, unlike their first trip to the dance studio, he felt unsure about what to say.

He'd seen her at church yesterday, and she'd been crying. Had they been good tears? Healing tears? Or had they been hurt tears? During the service, he hadn't let his focus linger on her for too long, and he hadn't been able to tell.

He'd looked for her afterward in the church hall, where the congregation gathered for coffee and donuts, but he hadn't found her. The Wise Widows she'd been sitting with during the service had told him that she'd left to retrieve Ivy from the childcare room.

Had she liked the music? Had the sermon spoken to her? Would she come back again next week?

He hoped her experience had been positive. Since learning that she hadn't been looking for a church, he'd been praying for her, and for her faith to grow, every day.

He slid into the driver's seat and turned on the car. "How was your weekend?"

"Good, thanks." She folded her hands in her lap. "Yours?"

"We played a new song at church."

"I know," she said, smiling. "I was there."

He nodded. "What did you think?"

"The music was great."

"And the rest of the service?"

She looked down at her hands. "I don't know. I'm still processing."

Processing was good. It meant she hadn't rejected the church or its message outright.

They rode in silence for a minute before Nate pulled up in front of the Sea Glass Inn, a two-story B and B that backed onto Sand Street Beach. The cedar-shingled structure was dusky in the evening light, sand dunes standing tall behind it.

"Pretty," Amanda said, getting out of the car. "This is where Bill and Irene are having their rehearsal dinner?"

"Yep, and from what I can tell, it's going to be almost as big as the reception. But Brett's been living here since last summer. He's a phenomenal chef."

As though he'd overheard them, Brett threw open the front door of the inn and waved them inside. "Hello, hello. Nice to see you again, Amanda. Welcome." He shook Amanda's hand and then slapped Nate on the back. "Can I take your coats?"

After Brett threw their coats on one of the blue sofas in the parlor, Nate watched as Amanda looked around the room, her gaze lingering on the sea-glass chandelier hanging from the ceiling, the carousel horse in the corner and the plate glass windows that overlooked the ocean. "This is beautiful," she said. "And that view!"

Brett strode over to the swinging door that separated the parlor from the dining room and pushed it open. "I can't take credit for the view, but the food's a different story. Irene and Bill asked me to give you two the full royal treatment, so—" he gave them a fancy hand flourish "—right this way."

They stepped into the dining room, where Brett had set two places at one of the long, farmhouse tables. It smelled fresh, with the savory scent of spices floating in the air, and Nate's stomach growled.

"Where's Valerie tonight?" he asked.

"She had to go to Boston last-minute for work," Brett said. "Chloe and Steve are watching the boys."

"And Laura and Jonathan?" he asked, referring to the property managers of the inn.

"Jonathan's mom's in town. She took them and the kids out for dinner. So sit! Get comfortable! I have five starters for you to try, and then five mains."

"Ooh!" Amanda's eyes lit up, and she rubbed her hands together. "What's on the menu?"

"First up, bacon-wrapped scallops. Then, crab-stuffed mushrooms, shrimp rolls, grilled oysters and lobster cakes."

"Whoa." Amanda's eyes popped wide open. "I'm going to have to roll myself out of here, aren't I?"

"For the mains, we've got cedar-planked salmon, ricotta-stuffed salmon rolls, crab-stuffed clams, shrimp pesto pasta and lobster ravioli."

"I'm drooling," Amanda said, patting her cheeks. "I'm literally drooling." She seemed lighter tonight, less burdened. Had attending church yesterday had anything to do with that? Nate sure hoped so.

"Brett's not just a great chef," he said, pulling out Amanda's chair. Her good mood was contagious. "He's also a bona fide hero. Ran into a burning house last fall and saved his girlfriend and her little brothers."

"She wasn't my girlfriend at the time," Brett protested.

"But pulling Dylan out of that fire sure didn't hurt your case."

"Nope." Brett chuckled. "But Amanda doesn't want to hear about all that."

"Oh, yes, I do," she said, picking up her water glass.

"He just found out he's being awarded a medal from the Carnegie Hero Fund Commission, which is pretty much the highest honor you can get for civilian heroism."

Her hand froze in midair, the water glass shaking.

Nate's stomach dropped. Something had upset her...but what?

Her gaze shifted between the two men, settling on Brett. "The Carnegie Medal?" she croaked. "You're getting the Carnegie Medal?"

"I am," he confirmed, frowning.

"When?"

Brett cocked his head to the side, giving her a concerned look. "Next month. Ceremony's in Boston. Why?"

"My husband's getting one then, too. Posthumously. I'm supposed to accept it on his behalf."

Chapter Seven

After Amanda dropped that little bomb, she shot to her feet and walked out, claiming she needed air.

Nate and Brett stared at each other.

"Um…" Brett scratched his ear.

Nate stood, knocking his knee on the underside of the table as his chair scraped the floor. "I'll go." This was, after all, what he did for a living. Listen to people. Comfort them. Gently remind them that God was sovereign, even in the hurt. Even in the hard. Even when the unimaginable happened.

He pushed through the swinging door into the parlor, which was empty. Through the window, a flicker of movement on the back porch caught his eye.

He went outside. Amanda was sitting at the top of the wooden steps that led down to the beach, staring at the water. It was cloudy this evening, so everything looked gray: the sky, the sand, the white-capped waves rolling in at high tide.

He sat beside her, leaving a few inches between them. She snuck a glance at him, then turned her face away. He waited, the sound of the surf soft and soothing in the background.

Lord, be with me. Give me the right words.

After a few moments, she glanced at him again. "Aren't you going to say something?"

"Do you want to talk about it?"

She shook her head.

"Then, no."

They went back to being quiet. After another minute of silence, and still staring at the waves, she said, "My sister-in-law nominated him for the medal. She didn't ask me before she did it. She was with him the day he died."

He paused before he spoke. "It's a big honor."

"It is, but I—I wish he hadn't done it. I don't think I can go to some ceremony where they call him a hero and praise him for it. Our daughter lost her father. That's not something I can celebrate."

"I understand."

She squinted at him, those big baby blues zinging with skepticism. "Do you?"

His heart squeezed. "My son's birthday is the anniversary of my wife's death. Of course I do."

Amanda wrapped her arms around her knees, hugging them to her chest. She was wearing jeans and a blue V-neck sweater with small white flowers embroidered around the neck. Her hair was loose, ruffling a little in the breeze. It was cool out here—should he offer to go get her jacket? "I hate it when people ask me what happened to him."

"I know. I do, too. But it gets easier to talk about it."

"Does it?"

He took off his glasses and cleaned them on his shirt, trying to ignore the instinct to lean in closer, to put his arm around her and draw her against his side. He was just a pastor giving his testimony to someone in need—nothing more, nothing less. So what if she was young and beautiful with eyes that blazed brighter than the sparkles on the waves? "Danielle got appendicitis when she was eight months pregnant."

Amanda took a sharp breath.

Although it was easier to talk about it now than it had been in the past, Nate wouldn't say it was easy. That gut punch of grief was still there.

"She woke me up in the middle of the night because her stomach hurt and she was worried about the baby. We went straight to Labor and Delivery, but everything with Hayden looked fine, so they said it was likely just indigestion. They took her to the ER just to be safe. By the time they got there, her blood pressure had plummeted to something like seventy over thirty and everyone took off running to get her hooked up and scanned. It was like a scene straight out of one of those medical dramas."

Amanda covered her mouth with her hand. "And…what? It was too late?"

"It wouldn't have been, if they'd called her OB right away. But they didn't. They did an ultrasound of her abdomen, but because of the baby, all her organs were kind of smooshed and pushed out of place. They couldn't tell what was going on. So, they gave her some IV drugs to help with the pain and sent us up to a room to wait until the morning, when they could call her obstetrician's office."

"Whoa. And she died before her doctor got there?"

Nate shook his head. "Doctor got there a little after nine, and he was livid. They should have called him right away, he said. They should have sent her back to L and D so she could be monitored more closely. He sent her for an MRI and called a couple of surgeons to come look at her scans, and one of them thought it was a kidney infection. He said they could treat it with IV antibiotics.

"By this time it was after two o'clock in the afternoon, and we'd been at the hospital for more than twelve hours. I'd spilled coffee on myself earlier, and Dani said I should go home to take a shower and change my clothes. The painkillers were pretty powerful, and she wasn't feeling too bad. So I left."

He'd told this story so many times, the emotion should have faded by now, but it hadn't. The guilt. The shock. The desolation.

Every time he relived that day—even now, twelve years later—he still had to box those feelings up and hand them over to God. Otherwise, he'd never get past it.

"She tried to call me after the other surgeon came in and said they needed to get her into surgery right away, but I was in the shower, so I missed her call. By the time I was done and called back, the nurse said she was already getting prepped for surgery.

"I rushed back there as fast as I could, but her appendix burst right before they got her on the table. They did their best, but it was too late. I never spoke with her again."

Amanda's knuckles were white where they were clutching her knees. "That's terrible. I'm so sorry."

"At first, I was mad at myself for leaving to take that shower. Like, really, who cared if I had coffee all over my shirt? But she told me to go. She wanted me to have a break. She didn't think that would be the last time we'd ever talk, and I didn't, either." If he could count all the nights he'd lain awake thinking about that, wishing he wasn't so clumsy and that he hadn't spilled that stupid beverage, it would amount to…too many. Way too many.

Because what would it have changed? Dani had known he loved her.

Still, even twelve years later, whenever he thought of her being alone at the end, of him not being there to comfort and care for her in those final moments, it made him feel like less of a man.

You were there, though, Lord. You were with her. So take this guilt from me. I know it's not where you want me to live.

"Then I was mad that I hadn't insisted the ER doctor call her OB right away. But honestly? I didn't know he hadn't. I didn't know he should've. You're there, and you trust that the doctors are doing what's best for you. You don't know any different."

"That's right," Amanda said fiercely, "you don't."

"Then I was mad that I was alone with this little person who needed his mother."

She nodded. "Yes. *Yes.* Exactly."

"And it was like, how could you do this to me, Dani? How could you do this to me, God?"

"Yes-s-s," she hissed.

"And I had to keep turning it over to God and turning it over to God. Because being angry all the time is exhausting."

"So you just…stopped being angry? Simple as that?"

He gave her a ghost of a smile. "As simple and as complicated as that."

"Oh, man." She hugged her knees tighter to her chest, turning away from him to look at the water. "You're a better person than I am."

"Nope," he assured her, "I've just been on this road a little longer."

They were quiet again. The wind picked up and Amanda tilted her face to the sky. The sun had set and the light was fading. "I think I've been nursing my anger at God because I'm afraid that if I let that go, I'm going to be furious at Pierce." Her eyes teared up. "And I don't want to be mad at him. I loved him. I still love him."

"You can love someone and be angry with them at the same time."

She pushed a hand through her hair. "He wasn't sick, like your wife. He drowned."

Nate stayed silent. They were members of a club no one wanted to join. But his loss meant he understood hers. And he also understood the value of patience.

"Three little girls got caught in a riptide."

"Did they survive?"

She wiped a tear from the corner of her eye. "Yes."

He waited for her to continue, and after a minute, she did. "He was a good swimmer. Fast. He got to them before anyone else."

"He saved them."

She nodded, still choked up. "He did. He chose them over Ivy. He chose them over *me*."

"Aww," Nate said gently, itching to put his arms around her, itching to take the edge off her hurt. "He didn't want to. He didn't *mean* to."

"I know he didn't mean to, but I'd never put the life of someone else's child ahead of Ivy's, and I just— I still can't believe that he did."

Then Nate did wrap an arm around her shoulder, because sometimes words weren't enough. "I'm sorry. That's hard."

He felt her next few breaths in the rise and fall of her shoulders, felt the hitch as she tried to get her emotions under control.

Finally, she put her face in her hands and let out a big breath. Then she looked up at him. "Thank you. I don't know what I thought you were going to say, but…thank you."

He lifted his shoulders. "You feel what you feel. And whatever it is, it's okay."

She pressed a hand to her cheek and studied him. "No Bible verses? No 'God has a plan'?"

Ah, he remembered those days. Well-meaning people

spouting well-meaning platitudes that had only made him feel worse. "Would that help?"

"No."

"Then, no."

She squinted at him. "You're not like any pastor I've ever met."

"I'll take that as a compliment."

"Good," she said, fiddling with her engagement ring. "You should."

It had been a long time since he'd surprised a woman, and it felt surprisingly good.

"Is there anything that *would* help right now?"

She sighed. "I don't know. But bacon-wrapped scallops probably wouldn't hurt."

He stood and offered her a hand getting to her feet. "Then let's do that."

"Let's." She smiled, and it was like sunshine on his face— warm and exhilarating. She squeezed his hand before letting it fall.

His heart squeezed, too.

Remember your role here, Pastor. Stay in your lane.

There would be age-appropriate women in Boston. Women who weren't angry. Women who weren't grieving. Women without a history of marrying real-life heroes…when Nate was anything but.

He had a sneaking suspicion, however, that his feelings for this particular woman might not fade just because they were inconvenient.

They might be here for keeps.

Chapter Eight

Amanda arrived at All That Jazz a half an hour early to speak with Ellen. An idea had sprouted in her mind when she'd first heard that Ellen was selling her business, and it had taken root over the last few weeks.

Pierce would have liked it—he'd always loved the fact that she kickboxed and had grown up practicing tae kwon do, and he'd wanted her to have lots of time with Ivy. Her brothers would like this idea, too.

Her mother? She'd hate it, but part of standing on her own two feet meant standing up for herself and fighting for what she wanted.

The one thing Amanda wasn't sure of was how to broach the subject with Irene.

Could she run both an exercise studio and the Candy Shack if she mapped everything out carefully? And if she couldn't, would she be able to stomach disappointing the one woman who'd always had her best interests in mind?

When Nate showed up, she was mulling over everything she'd learned during her conversation with Ellen. Taking over the studio would be risky, but thanks to the money Pierce had left her, it was doable. The studio's gross revenue was good, and Ellen would include all the furniture, fixtures and equipment as part of the sale. She'd also provide three months of training and mentoring, if Amanda wanted it, and make sure her part-time instructors would stay on after the studio changed hands if Amanda was interested in keeping the dance classes going.

"You're distracted tonight," Nate said, as they warmed up by swaying to the music. He was in athletic clothes again, and he'd already taken off his shoes.

"Sorry." She toed off her own shoes and deposited them over by the wall, then walked back to where he was standing in her stockinged feet, skating a little on the freshly waxed floor. "Just thinking about something."

"Whoa, careful there, Gretzky." He threw out his hands as though to catch her, although she was perfectly steady on her feet.

"Who?"

His jaw dropped. "You've never heard of Wayne Gretzky?"

She laughed. "You're so gullible."

"So you *have* heard of him?"

"Greatest hockey player of all time, right? Like Tom Brady is for football?"

Nate slapped a hand to his heart. "Oh, Brady. How we miss thee."

"You're a Patriots fan, are you?"

"Why do you sound surprised?"

"I don't know. I mean, a guitar-playing pastor who likes football? It's…unusual."

He smiled. "It's really not. How many pastors do you know outside of a church setting?"

"Uh, one. You."

"There you go. We're just people. We've all got interests and hobbies that aren't related to the church. But, anyway, what were you distracted by? Not what we were talking about the other night, I hope?"

A little zing of happiness shot through her. He cared about her. He wanted her to work through her grief, not because it would make it more comfortable for him to be around her, but so that she could live a full life.

"No," she assured him, "although talking to you about what happened actually did help. But this is something different. Something kind of crazy. But it would give me and Ivy some real roots here on Cape Cod."

"Roots are good."

She glanced at Ellen and bit her lip. "Yeah, I just— I don't know."

"Have you prayed about it?"

She nodded. Since that day in church, she actually *had* been praying again, and it felt…good. Soothing. Like sliding her feet into sheepskin slippers on a cold day.

"I'm happy to hear that," he said. "Hopefully you'll get some clarity soon."

Ellen started a new song. They'd pretty much mastered the simple box step over the last few weeks, and now they were working on the traveling and turning box step. They started practicing, and Amanda was definitely sliding around a little in her stockings. "Should we put on our shoes?"

"You can," he said, his brow furrowed as he concentrated on his steps. "I'll leave mine off so I don't hurt you."

She decided to forgo the footwear and soldier on.

Wrong decision.

Because as her left foot went to the side into their turn, it slipped. She tightened her grip on Nate to try to stop her fall, but all she accomplished was pulling him off balance.

As he went down on his back, she tripped over him, falling forward and landing hard on her right elbow and the heel of her left hand.

"Ow," she cried, a sharp pain tearing through her when she tried to push herself up.

"Ugh," Nate groaned.

Ellen stopped the music and ran over to them, wringing her hands. "Oh, no. Are you okay?"

Nate sat up, pressing his hand to his tailbone. "Oh, man, that hurts." He sounded winded, but immediately turned his attention to Amanda. "How're you doing there? Can you sit up?"

She tried again to push off her left hand, gasping as a wave of intense pain made her stomach roll.

"Don't move," Nate ordered. "What hurts?"

She sucked in another breath, trying not to be sick. "My wrist. And my elbow."

"Not your neck or your head?"

"No."

"I'm going to lift you up, okay?"

She nodded, and he pulled her up from under her armpits until she could shift her legs enough to sit.

"Should I call an ambulance?" Ellen asked, her face pinched.

"I just need a minute." Amanda closed her eyes, waiting for the pain to subside. It didn't.

"Take your time." Nate's voice was low and reassuring. Then he turned to Ellen. "Do you have an ice pack? Maybe two or three?"

"Let me check." The older woman rushed off to take stock of her ice-pack supply.

"I'm sorry," he said. "I was trying to stop your fall, but I took us both down instead."

"*I'm* sorry. I'm the one who slipped." She tried to shake out her wrist, which made it hurt a thousand times worse. "Ow, ow, ow."

He scooted closer. "Let me see."

"Don't touch. It hurts."

He winced at what he saw. "It's already swelling up."

"Great." Her and her brilliant ideas. She should have known that dancing in stockinged feet would turn into a disaster. Maybe it was a sign that taking over this studio would be more than she could handle.

"Do you want her to call an ambulance?" Nate asked.

"I'm not an invalid. No." But her wrist was definitely throbbing.

"We should probably get you to the ER or an urgent care, though."

She gave a heavy sigh. "Probably." Her wrist might be broken.

"Let me get our shoes."

Ellen came back with some ice packs while Nate hobbled over to grab their shoes. Ellen insisted that he sit in one of the folding chairs along the wall to put his own shoes on, then she came over and helped Amanda into her shoes and onto her feet.

"Are you sure you don't want an ambulance?" the studio owner asked again, back to wringing her hands.

Nate shot a questioning glance at her, and Amanda shook her head. "No, we're good, Ellen."

"But you're going to see a doctor, aren't you?"

"I'll take her right now," Nate said.

They limped outside and got into his car. A few minutes later, they were in Cape Cod Memorial Hospital's ER waiting room, which was packed. They checked in, then found a pair of seats in a quiet corner.

"I'd better call Irene," Amanda said. "This is going to take all night." But she couldn't get her phone out of her pocket. Her elbow hurt too much to bend her right arm and she couldn't even think about using her left wrist.

"I'll do it."

He took out his own cell and made the call, informing Irene about what had happened, then putting it on speaker and holding it up to Amanda's ear so she could ask if Irene would be willing to keep Ivy overnight.

"Don't worry about a thing. We'll have a great time here. But I'm going to have to call your mother. If you broke your wrist, you're going to need some help."

Anxiety shot through her. Her mom was the last person she wanted to see right now, and Amanda had no doubt that as soon as Irene made the call, her mom would hop on a plane. "No, we don't know anything yet. Please don't call her."

"I could call Caroli—"

"No!" Amanda's anxiety spiraled into full-blown panic. Nate's eyebrows shot up, and the people sitting next to her gave her a serious case of side-eye. "I don't want to see her, Irene. Promise me you won't call her."

Irene sighed. "You should listen to her. Talk to her. There are things you need to—"

"No!"

"She feels just as—"

"Don't. Please. She doesn't. How could she?"

"He was her brother," Irene said gently.

"And she was right there!" Amanda cried. "If she cared that much, she would have helped him—tried to help him! But she didn't. She didn't! And now he's gone and the stupid medal they want to give him won't change anything!"

"Shh," Irene said. "I won't call her. I'm sorry I brought it up. Can you give the phone back to Nate?"

Nate took the phone off speaker and put it back to his ear.

He spoke to Irene in low tones, but Amanda wasn't paying attention to what he said. Wasn't paying attention to the stares of the people around her or the tears trailing down her cheeks, either.

She was thinking about that day, that phone call and then the three horrible days she'd waited—hoping against hope, praying that Pierce had somehow defied all the odds and hung on—for the Coast Guard to recover his body.

In those three days, she'd lost eight pounds from the stress. She'd tossed and turned for hours only to be jolted awake by the icy hand of panic as soon as she'd fallen asleep. She'd had to hire a full-time caregiver to come to the house and take care of Ivy because she'd been too upset to do much of anything herself.

Caroline had tried to talk to her then, but Amanda had blocked her calls and texts and refused to let her in the house. At the funeral, her brothers had circled around her and kept everyone away. And then, her mother had bundled her onto a plane and taken her back to California.

Her mother-in-law had tried to hand the phone to Caroline a couple of times while she was video-chatting with Ivy, but Amanda had always swooped right in and ended those calls. Miyoko had taken the hint quickly enough.

There was nothing Caroline could ever say that would make things right between them.

The same way she'd never understand why Pierce had sacrificed himself for a stranger's children, she'd never forgive Caroline for staying out of the water that day.

Never.

Nate got up, limped over to the check-in window, came back with a box of tissues and gently deposited them on her lap. "Thought you might need some of these."

She stared at the tissues for a moment, tried to dip her

right hand down and snag one without jostling her injured elbow but failed miserably. Then she started laughing. It wasn't normal laughter, either. No, this was desperate laughter, frantic laughter.

Laughter that made the tears already running down her face flow faster.

"Need help?" The concerned look on Nate's face confirmed that she was a total mess.

She took a few deep breaths in through her nose and out through her mouth. "It hurts too much to even pick up a Kleenex."

He plucked one out of the box. "I'll get it for you." Realizing that she couldn't do anything with it, he mimed dabbing at her face. "Do you want me to…?"

She nodded, feeling both helpless and foolish. "Yes, please."

Softly and carefully, he dabbed the tears off her cheeks. And her insides were obviously a tangled twist of confusion, because even as he cleared away the tears she'd cried over another man, she wanted to lean into his touch.

Instead, she forced herself to sit back in her chair. "Irene's right, isn't she? I'm going to need help."

"Yeah," he said, sighing. "I think you are."

Nate had only bruised his tailbone. The doctor had advised ice, rest and sitting on a pillow. Amanda hadn't been quite as fortunate.

Although her elbow was merely badly bruised, her wrist was broken. The doctor had given her a splint for now; in a few days, once the swelling came down, they'd put her in a cast, which she'd have to wear for at least six weeks.

Right up until the wedding.

Which meant no more dance lessons. No more holding Amanda in his arms.

It was for the best. His two left feet had struck again, and way more catastrophically than at junior prom.

Amanda was a single mom to a little girl who couldn't dress herself, feed herself or take a bath on her own. The two of them had no family here on Cape Cod, and Amanda wouldn't let Irene call her mother or her sister-in-law.

He took off his glasses and rubbed his eyes. It was late—past midnight—and they were still waiting for Amanda to be discharged.

She'd tried to get him to go home after his exam was done, but there was no chance he'd leave a woman he cared about alone at a hospital ever again. Zero. None.

Even if that woman was just a friend.

She was half-reclined in the hospital bed with her eyes closed. He knew she wasn't sleeping, but at least she was getting some rest. He still couldn't believe he'd tripped her. Yes, she'd slipped first, but for once, couldn't he have been coordinated? Couldn't he have caught her instead of compounding the problem by pulling her down?

Brett Richardson wouldn't have broken Valerie's wrist if he'd found himself in a similar predicament. In fact, the younger man had broken his own fingers punching out a window during a fire in order to keep Valerie's little brother safe.

Based on what Nate knew of Amanda's late husband, he was sure that Pierce would have done everything in his power to take the hit if he'd been in Nate's place.

Just once, Nate would like to be the hero. The guy who swooped in and set things right rather than the one holding the bag when everything went wrong, unintentional though it might be.

"Penny for your thoughts," Amanda said, her eyes open now, watching him.

He rubbed the back of his neck. "I wish I'd been able to catch you."

She laughed. "You and me both."

"Are you hungry?" The wait had been long, and since they were in the ER and not the hospital proper, they hadn't been offered dinner. He'd gotten up a few times to forage from the vending machine, bringing back pretzels, peanut-butter crackers, Gatorade and a pack of licorice.

"No, all those snacks should tide me over until breakfast."

"You'd think they'd have healthier options here, wouldn't you?"

She nodded, her eyes glued to his. "You would."

Suddenly, the air felt charged, and his throat felt thick.

One beat passed, their gazes locked.

Another.

He could see her pulse flickering against the soft skin of her neck, and all he could think about was getting closer to her and…

He tore his gaze away and said a quick prayer. *Let the words of my mouth, and the meditation of my heart, be acceptable in thy sight, O Lord, my strength, and my redeemer.*

He needed to keep his feelings for her in check, otherwise he wouldn't just want to be *a* hero; he'd want to be *her* hero. And they'd both already acknowledged that getting romantically involved with each other would be a bad idea.

"Do you want me to drop you off at home after this? Or at Irene's?"

"Home, I guess. I'd hate to wake her up at this hour."

"Want me to come get you in the morning to go pick up Ivy?"

"Would you?"

"Of course. It's my fault you're in this mess."

She shook her head. "It's not your fault."

"I'll help you with her as much as I can, but we both know there are some things that a woman should take care of."

Amanda frowned. "Irene's right. I need to call my mom."

"What about your mother-in-law? She's closer, isn't she?"

"I don't think we could communicate well enough without…"

"Caroline?" he asked, guessing.

She nodded.

"Your sister-in-law," he said, remembering what she'd said about how she'd met Pierce. "Your best friend."

"*Former* best friend."

"She was with him the day he died?"

"She didn't even dip her toe in the water to go help him," she said, her voice strangled. "She stood there and watched him drown—her brother, the love of my life."

His heart ached for her. She was only twenty-six; she had so much life left to live. Was she going to shut herself off for a whole decade like he had?

"And you can't forgive her?"

The look she shot him was pure challenge. "Could you?" Then she sat up straighter in her hospital bed as though something important had just occurred to her. "And don't answer like a pastor. Answer like a normal human being."

Like he was some lofty spiritual being instead of a flesh-and-blood man with his own flaws and failings.

In truth, most people saw him like that. And they held him a little bit separate. Kept him a little bit apart.

It was lonely, and he'd been alone in his commitment to the ministry for a long time. Yes, he had his father and Hayden, but it would be nice to have a partner he could confide in. Someone who knew the man he was beneath all the pastoral trappings. Someone who loved him whether he had a role in the church or not. "Pastors *are* normal human beings."

"You know what I mean."

"I don't have all the answers, Amanda."

She looked down at her hands. "I wish someone did."

"Someone does. Jesus. The rest of us are all just doing our best to figure it out as we go."

Once Amanda realized that she'd need to ask her mother for help, she sucked it up and called her from the hospital. It might be late here in Massachusetts, but in California, it was only a little after nine.

"It's too late to catch a red-eye," her mom said, "but there's a seven-thirty flight that should get me into Boston by late afternoon. As long as the line at the rental-car agency isn't too long and the traffic isn't too bad, I should be there in time to put Ivy to bed."

"Thanks, Mom."

"Of course, baby. Is there someone who can help you while I'm in the air?"

"Nate's going to drive me to Irene's in the morning." Amanda glanced at him, and he nodded. "He'll help."

"Ooh." Her mom's voice brightened. "And who's Nate?"

"Bill's son. The pastor." Although she only saw it out of the corner of her eye, she was pretty sure he clenched his jaw as he looked away. What was that all about?

"Right. Well, you make sure to put him to work, princess. Not just with Ivy, but with that wedding shower, too. That wrist won't heal itself."

The wedding shower was coming up fast, but fortunately Amanda had already ordered all the supplies and didn't have much left to do beyond setting everything up on the day itself.

"All right, Mom. I'll see you tomorrow."

She was discharged soon after, and Nate drove her home, then walked her up to her door. The salty sea air smelled richer at night, the sound of the waves lapping the shore behind her house louder.

Amanda peeked up at the sky as Nate rummaged through her purse for her keys. She was grateful she'd moved here. In Los Angeles, the light pollution and the smog had been so bad that you could only see a small handful of stars at night…and sometimes only the very brightest of the planets. The night sky in Boston, although not as smoggy, had been much the same.

Nate unlocked her front door and opened it for her. "What time should I come back in the morning?"

"The Candy Shack opens at nine, so around eight, maybe? That should give us plenty of time to pick up Ivy before Irene needs to be at work. Unless you want to stay over. I have a guest room you're welcome to use."

"Oh, uh…" His forehead creased with discomfort. "Thank you. That's really generous, but…people talk, and I should go."

If her wrist hadn't been broken and her other arm bruised, she could have smacked herself. Of course, people talked. He was a pastor. And no matter how pure her intentions, it wouldn't look good if anyone saw him sleeping over at a single woman's house. "Sure," she said lightly.

"Do you need help, uh, getting ready for bed?"

She shook her head, almost smiling at the uneasiness on his face. "I'll just sleep in my clothes tonight."

"Solid plan, my friend," he said, backing away. "Solid plan."

His relief in getting away from her was palpable, and although on one hand it was amusing, it hurt a little, too. It was embarrassing enough that she'd put her attraction out there in the first place…even if it had only been to warn him away. Did he really have to remind her—right now, when she was injured and exhausted—that the feeling wasn't mutual? That he only saw her as a friend?

Oh, well. What exactly did she want? Despite her years on the pageant circuit, she wasn't one of those women who thrived on male attention. The fact that Nate wasn't romantically interested in her should be a relief.

And yet, as she climbed the stairs to her bedroom and tried to get comfortable in her bed, she couldn't help but wish that their timing had been better. That they'd met when Ivy was older, and when he wasn't on the cusp of moving, and when she'd had time to move beyond what had happened to Pierce.

Maybe one day she'd be ready to open her heart again.

Alas, she thought as she slipped into sleep, *today is not that day.*

Chapter Nine

The sound of the doorbell woke Nate early the next morning. He rolled over to check his alarm—it was just after seven— and groaned in pain. His tailbone was on fire.

Sitting up, he grabbed two Tylenols off his nightstand and washed them down with a mouthful of water. Who on earth was at the door at seven o'clock on a Friday morning?

He quickly got dressed, catching the scent of coffee and the sound of a light female laugh. What was going on? His dad hadn't mentioned anything about entertaining friends this morning.

"Dad?" he called out as he carefully navigated his way down the stairs.

"In the kitchen!" his father called back.

When he entered the kitchen, he stopped. Blinked.

Hayden, his dad and his in-laws were all grinning at him.

"Surprise!"

His mother-in-law, Cheryl, who was slim and small with corkscrew curls that were naturally going gray, was even doing jazz hands.

"Wow." Nate rubbed his jaw. He needed to shower and shave and drink some coffee. A lot of coffee. He was still so tired he was half-wondering if this was a dream. "It's great to see you, but—" he squinted at his dad, who held up his palms in a *beats me* gesture "—what are you doing here?"

"We're going on a five-day bicycle tour of Nantucket and Martha's Vineyard with our friends, the Barclays," Cheryl explained, her eyes bright, "and we thought we'd fly up early and surprise you and Hayden!"

His in-laws were active people, so the bike tour wasn't a shock, but they weren't in the habit of dropping by from Texas unannounced. Generally, twice a year they rented a beach house, stayed for a week and made a vacation out of it. "That's fantastic," Nate said, finally shaking off his surprise enough to kiss Cheryl on the cheek and give Tim a hearty handshake. "Which flight did you take?"

"The six o'clock out of Houston. It got us into Boston at eleven, and we stayed at an airport hotel last night so we could hit the road bright and early this morning and say hello to this one—" she gave Hayden's cheek an affectionate pat "—before school."

Hayden beamed at his grandma. "They're going to take me for ice cream this afternoon!"

"And dinner, Hayden," Tim added. "Wherever you want."

Like his wife, Tim was going gray gracefully, and he always looked ready to step out on the golf course. They were a happy, elegant couple, and Danielle used to talk all the time about how she wanted to be just like them when she grew up.

"If you'd given us a heads-up, I could have talked to the school and gotten Hayden the day off," Nate said, "but he's got a science test today that he really shouldn't miss."

"We actually planned it this way," Tim said. "We drove down here to pick you up and take you to Boston for the day. I've arranged lunch with one of the professors from Harvard. That way, you can get the lay of the land."

Hayden looked at him quizzically. Nate hadn't thought

to warn Tim that Hayden didn't know about the PhD program yet.

Nate wouldn't lie to his son if he asked about it, but he really didn't want to tell him about the move until the end of the school year. Tim, a Harvard alum himself, was a nonresident member of the Harvard Club of Boston, and he'd taken Nate there as a guest a number of times over the years. Hopefully, Hayden would assume this lunch date was just one more of the same.

At any rate, Nate had more pressing concerns. "Today?" he asked, rubbing the back of his neck, acutely aware that Amanda needed him to get back to her house before too long so they could retrieve Ivy from Irene's. "You booked it for today?"

Tim's eyebrows slammed together. "Is that a problem?"

Nate glanced at his father. "Did you tell them anything about what happened last night?"

Cheryl's gaze whipped back and forth between them while his father stroked his mustache and shook his head. "What happened last night?" she demanded.

"Dad and Ms. Kobayashi went dancing," Hayden said helpfully, pushing his glasses up his nose. "They stayed out *really* late."

Cheryl's chin wobbled. "Dancing?"

"She's the maid of honor in Dad and Irene's wedding," Nate quickly assured her. "We're trying to perfect our moves."

"Oh."

"Except Dad's terrible," Hayden added gleefully, "and he broke her wrist!"

Both Cheryl's and Tim's eyes went wide.

"Hayden!" Nate massaged his temple. "It's not funny. It's going to be hard for her to take care of Ivy now that she's injured."

"Who's Ivy?" Cheryl asked.

"Ms. K's a widow like Dad, and Ivy's her daughter. She's almost three. And cute. I've been babysitting her a lot. Dad and Ms. K spend *a lot* of time together."

Even Tim's eyebrows went up at that. Cheryl, meanwhile, looked stricken. "She's a member of my congregation," Nate said, trying to explain. "She comes to the grief group on Tuesday nights."

"We've been over to their house for dinner," Hayden went on. "It's right on the water. Super nice. They're kinda rich, aren't they, Dad?"

What had gotten into that kid? Couldn't he tell his grandmother was getting upset? "Hayden, go make sure you've got everything you need for school in your backpack."

"I do."

Nate gave him a tight smile. "Go check again." He caught his father's eye and tilted his head toward Hayden. "Why don't you help supervise, Dad?"

His dad took the hint, and they both left the room. Once they were alone, his in-laws focused their attention on him.

"Exactly how well do you know this woman?" Cheryl asked, her voice rising. She'd always been quick to heat up, but quick to cool down, too, once she'd had a chance to think things through.

Tim placed his hand on Cheryl's forearm. "Now, Sherry," he murmured, calling her by her nickname.

She shook him off. "No, I think we deserve to know what kind of women he's exposing our grandson to."

"Cheryl," Nate said. "You've got the wrong idea."

At the same time, Tim put his arm around her. "Sweetheart, it's been twelve years. Nate's a grown man. This is none of our business."

Cheryl leveled her gaze on Nate. "You promised us you wouldn't forget about Danielle."

"I have never, not for one second, forgotten about Danielle," he said firmly. "I don't know what that was all about with Hayden, but Amanda and I are just friends."

Cheryl stared at him for a moment, sizing him up. Then she sighed, looking at least somewhat mollified. "Amanda. That's not an Asian name like Kobayashi."

Nate sat, winced and stood back up. "She's not Asian. Her late husband's parents emigrated from Japan."

"Oh, that's interesting. But what's wrong with your back?"

"We really did have a mishap last night at the dance studio. I bruised my tailbone."

"Is that why you don't want to drive to Boston for lunch?" Tim asked. "Too uncomfortable to sit in the car for a two-hour drive?"

"I'd be happy to sit through some discomfort to go to lunch with you and your professor friend, Tim, but Amanda actually did break her wrist, and I promised I'd help her wrangle her daughter until her mother arrives from California."

Cheryl tapped her chin. "When's her mother arriving?"

"Later today."

"And Hayden babysits her daughter?"

Nate nodded. "She's the little girl he rescued off the jetty. He told you about that, right?"

"Oh! No wonder you've been over there for dinner. What a close call that was! It's so dangerous out there when the tide comes in."

"Slippery," Tim added, a furrow between his eyes. "And don't get me started on those crevices between the rocks."

"I know," Nate said. "We never go out there unless it's a calm day."

"Is Hayden still taking swimming lessons?" Cheryl asked.

"Of course. He's mastered the strokes, though, so he's in the swim club at the Y now. He's got his eye on the junior lifeguard program the National Park Service puts on in Wellfleet in the summer, although he's got to be thirteen to qualify for that."

"Are they worried about sharks this year?"

Nate shrugged. The waters around Cape Cod were a known gathering spot for great white sharks. In fact, the iconic movie *Jaws* had been filmed on Martha's Vineyard, which was only a forty-five-minute ferry ride away. "No more than usual. There haven't been any shark attacks in the last few years."

Cheryl gave a little shudder. "If anything were to ever happen to Hayden…"

"He's a great swimmer, Cheryl. And you know that I swim in the ocean all the time, and I've never seen a shark."

"Is that little girl taking swimming lessons? Your friend should enroll her in a survival swim class. I've heard those are the best for kids that age."

"I'll ask her. I need to drive over there after I drop Hayden at school and help her pick up her daughter from Irene's."

"Why don't you let us take Hayden to school?" Tim asked. "Give your tailbone a break."

Nate wanted to talk to Hayden about why he'd been exaggerating how much time Nate and Amanda spent together to his grandparents, but he also wanted to make sure that Tim and Cheryl got lots of time with their grandson while they were in town. "That'd be great. But I'd appreciate it if you'd keep the talk about Harvard to a minimum. I haven't told him about the move yet."

"Of course," Tim said. "Sorry about that. When are you planning to tell him?"

Nate had been back and forth about this a lot in his mind. "I don't think it's a good idea to tell him while school's still in session. He'll tell all his friends and it'll turn into a giant pity party. And I don't want to spoil my dad's wedding for him, either, so probably after that."

"All right." Tim dipped his chin in acquiescence. "We'll keep it quiet."

"I'm going to run upstairs for a quick shower, but you're welcome to come back here and relax after you've dropped him off."

"Ask your friend if she'd like my help with her daughter today," Cheryl said. "That way, you boys can still head up to Boston for lunch."

He'd ask. He couldn't imagine that Amanda would want his mother-in-law hanging around all day, but he'd leave that choice up to her.

Amanda stopped walking on her way to Nate's car. "Your mother-in-law?" she repeated. "The one who slapped you?"

It was a crisp, sunny morning, the kind that, if Pierce had been alive, they would have taken turns going for a run on the beach. Although it was mid-May, it wasn't breaking sixty degrees these days until the afternoon, so the sand would be cool, smooth and refreshing on the bottom of her feet as she ran.

Her wrist and elbow hurt, but the pain was manageable. The worst thing this morning was the itch under her splint she couldn't scratch.

"That was one time," Nate said mildly, "and there were extenuating circumstances."

She wrinkled her forehead. "Why would she volunteer to help watch Ivy?"

"I think she's just trying to be helpful. My father-in-law

wants to take me up to Boston to meet a professor friend of his from the divinity school, but I said I couldn't go because I needed to help you. Plus, Hayden made kind of a big deal about you and I spending time together, so she's probably curious about you, too."

Amanda chewed her lip. "Why would Hayden make a big deal out of us being friends?"

Nate opened the car door for her, and she ducked her head as she got in. "I don't know. I need to talk to him about it. It was strange."

He came around to the driver's side and eased into his seat while trying to hide a grimace. "Tailbone hurts?" Amanda asked.

"Yep," he groaned, gritting out the word.

Maybe she should take his mother-in-law up on her offer. Nate was obviously in no condition to be chasing around after Ivy, and he'd been right last night when he'd said that there would be aspects of caring for a little girl that would be better handled by a woman.

Plus, she didn't want to be the reason he couldn't go to lunch with one of his future professors. He'd done so much for her over the past few weeks, and she really hadn't recip-rocated at all. Accepting the help of a stranger so he could have the day to prepare for his PhD program would be the absolute least she could do.

"She knows we're just friends, right?"

"Yeah, I made that clear."

"Does she like kids? Is she a good grandma?"

"The best," Nate said, glancing over at her. "Aside from my mom, God rest her soul, Cheryl's literally the best."

They made it to Irene's quickly—outside of tourist sea-son, there was never any traffic in Wychmere Bay—and Ivy sprang up from her seat at the kitchen table. "Mama!"

she cried, running over to Amanda and throwing herself at her legs.

"Gentle, chickadee." Amanda laughed as she steadied them both. "Mommy's got a cast now, too."

Ivy looked up and squealed in delight at the sight of Amanda's splint. "We twins!"

"Yes, we are."

Ivy noticed Nate and beamed at him. "Haybee's dad! You here, too!"

"Hi, Ivy." He gave her a little wave, looking pleased that she was so happy to see him.

"Where Haybee?"

"He's at school."

"Haybee drawed a picture on my cast." She thrust her little arm out so Nate could see the colorful bouquet Hayden had sketched out. "Bootiful fowlers!"

Nate smiled. "Very beautiful."

"Mama, I eating pancakes now."

"Sounds great," Amanda replied, turning her attention to Irene. "How'd you two do last night?"

Ivy's presence didn't seem to have ruffled the older woman in the least; Irene was dressed in gray slacks and a stylish white shirt, her bright red lipstick already in place. "We did just fine here, didn't we, Miss Ivy?" Ivy gave her a big, syrupy nod, and Irene turned back to Amanda and Nate. "And you? You two won't be able to keep up with this one if you're both injured. Did you call your mother?"

Amanda nodded. "She'll be here tonight."

Irene briskly wiped her hands on a dish towel. "I'd offer to lend you a hand today, but I don't have anyone to watch the store."

"It's all right. Nate's mother-in-law is going to come over and help."

Irene tossed Nate a raised eyebrow. "Cheryl's in town?"

"They surprised me this morning. They're starting a biking tour of Martha's Vineyard on Monday. They're just here for the weekend."

"Well, well, well." Irene steepled her fingers, the hint of a smile playing on her lips. "Interesting."

Irene's reaction worried Amanda. She was already nervous about this whole setup, but she didn't want to ask Nate to miss his lunch. "Why? Don't you like her?"

"I like her just fine, young lady." That hint of a smile widened into a Cheshire cat–like grin. "Now we get to see what she thinks of *you*."

Although Amanda recognized that Irene was goading her, she couldn't deny that the comment lit a fire under her. She might not be ready for a relationship, but she suddenly had a burning desire to prove to Nate's mother-in-law that, if circumstances were different, she could be the kind of woman Nate and Hayden needed in their lives.

Chapter Ten

"So." Tim tapped his Harvard class ring on the steering wheel as they sat in a traffic snarl in Back Bay, the ritzy neighborhood in Boston where the Harvard Club was located. Driving here required navigating through a maze of cobblestone streets, rotaries and one-way roads.

It was cherry-blossom season, so the view was spectacular—pink petals floating through the air like puffs of cotton candy—but Nate would never want to live downtown like this. Although he was sure the brownstone buildings were beautiful inside, they were so packed together that there was no room to breathe.

Tim pulled to a stop at a red light and glanced at Nate. "What did you think?"

Nate shifted in his seat in an attempt to ease the pain in his tailbone, bumping his knee on the glove box in the process. "Ow." He rubbed his leg. "It was…educational."

Tim popped an eyebrow. "Meaning?"

"Some of the research he was talking about was a little out there, wasn't it?"

Tim laughed and cuffed Nate on the shoulder. "You're not in Kansas anymore, my boy. Or, in your case, that teeny tiny church."

"Right," Nate said slowly. But the thought of dedicating

the next five years of his life to exploring that kind of research was... He wasn't sure. He just wasn't sure.

Tim gave him a sideways glance. "You said your goal is to teach. Has that changed?"

"No." Danielle had always thought he'd make a good teacher, and Nate figured it would be a lot like preaching, just in the classroom, where there was more discussion to be had.

Actually, it would probably be more like the Wise Widowhood meetings than anything else, and those meetings were one of his favorite parts of the week.

The only question mark was the subject matter. Based on what Tim's professor colleague had said at lunch, as a teaching assistant, he might have to present on niche topics like Religious Perspectives on Psychedelics or The Intersection of Christianity and Ecospirituality. He liked to study scripture as much as the next member of the clergy, but over the years he'd observed that the more you tried to fancy up your faith, the easier it was to lose.

"Well," his father-in-law said, "you get a degree from Harvard, you can teach anywhere you want."

"Right," Nate said again.

Tim turned onto Massachusetts Avenue and began driving across the Harvard Bridge into Cambridge. Since they were already so close to campus, they were going to poke around Harvard Square and take a look at the outside of the graduate-student apartment buildings.

As they crossed the bridge, the Charles River sparkled in the sunlight, a pair of rowers sculling across the water in a two-man shell. The trees were lush and green on both sides of the river, and Nate could picture taking Hayden for bike rides on the Esplanade on spring and summer afternoons.

Hayden would like it in Boston, wouldn't he? The history, the parks, the subway system—there was a lot here for a kid to explore. And it wasn't *that* far from Wychmere Bay. They could always drive down for a visit if they started feeling homesick.

"Is this about that woman? Your friend Amanda?"

Nate turned to his father-in-law in surprise. "No."

"I know Sherry reacted badly at first, but we want you to be happy, Nate. And Dani would want that, too."

Nate swallowed, feeling oddly touched. "Thanks, Tim. That means a lot to me. But I meant what I said this morning. Amanda and I aren't dating. We're just friends."

"Hmm." His father-in-law tapped his ring on the steering wheel again. "Maybe you *should* date her. It's obvious that Hayden approves."

Nate groaned. "I don't know what got into him this morning. That was bizarre."

Tim opened his mouth, then hesitated. They were driving through Kendall Square now, home of a wide variety of technology start-ups founded by alums of MIT.

"You can say it," Nate told him. "Don't walk on eggshells around me."

"You might think he can't miss what he never had, but he can. And I think he does. Mothers…they're special. Even for teenage boys who rebel against it sometimes, you don't get that kind of love anywhere else."

Nate sat with that for a moment, the truth of it like an anvil on his chest. Losing his own mother had been hard, and he'd been almost thirty. He'd tried his best to fill that hole for his son, but he was just one person. One man.

"I've always done my best to keep Dani's memory alive for him."

"We know you have, and we appreciate it. That, and keeping us in your life. We couldn't have asked for a better son-in-law, or a better father for our grandson. We're proud of you and everything you've done raising Hayden."

"Thanks." Nate's throat tightened, and he coughed to clear it. He'd been up late last night, so it was no wonder his emotions were close to the surface today.

"Do you like this woman?"

"Her husband's only been gone a year and a half."

Tim's lips twitched. "That's not what I asked."

Might as well lay his cards on the table, since his father-in-law seemed to have guessed how he felt, anyway. "She's only twenty-six, Tim."

His father-in-law chuckled, slowing the car to look for street parking. "So?"

"She was barely a teenager when Hayden was born. Don't you think it would be a little weird for me to start dating someone her age?"

"You're thirty-nine, Nate. Not ninety."

Yes, but he'd done enough premarital counseling to know that a thirteen-year age difference was significant. "Age is a big part of compatibility."

Tim snorted. "Cheryl's eight years younger than me, and we're coming up on thirty-seven years of marriage. Age is just a number."

"But you've seen those studies, right? Married couples with the same birth year are way less likely to get divorced than people with even a five-year age gap. And we're talking over a decade here."

Tim shot him a skeptical look as he pulled into a metered spot in front of a little gray stone church. "You're worried about divorce before you've even gone on a date with this woman?"

As part of his PhD program, Nate would be serving as a teaching assistant for an Intro to Religion class this coming fall. "Wouldn't it look bad for a TA to be dating someone so much younger?"

"She's twenty-six, she's been married and she has a daughter. This isn't a wide-eyed freshman we're talking about." His father-in-law narrowed his eyes, which were gray...just like Danielle's. "What's really going on?"

"Hayden and I are moving."

"Months from now. Try again."

Nate gazed out the car window at the little church, its spears and spires and stained glass, and sighed. "I broke her wrist, Tim. I doubt she's looking at me as a hot romantic prospect."

"It was an accident. Happens to the best of us."

Nate took off his glasses and rubbed his eyes. "It happens to me a lot, though. I'm clumsy. Careless. People get hurt."

Tim frowned. "I wouldn't call you careless. A little uncoordinated, maybe, but not careless."

"That's not what Cheryl said the day she slapped me."

Tim pulled on the collar of his golf shirt. "That was the grief talking. You know that."

"If I hadn't spilled coffee on myself in the hospital that day—"

"You might've been there to kiss Dani before they took her back for surgery," Tim interrupted, "but that's it, Nate. You didn't hurt her. You didn't give her appendicitis. It wasn't your fault, and you being there wouldn't have changed the outcome."

"I should've done more to get the ER doctors to call her OB."

"Hindsight's twenty-twenty, son, and what happened to Danielle is still not your fault."

Nate scrubbed his hands over his face. He knew all of that. Intellectually, he knew all of that, but it never fully sunk in.

"Amanda's husband—he was a hero. Saved three little girls from drowning. That's how he died."

Tim stared at him for a moment, then took the car keys out of the ignition and opened his door. "Come on. Let's walk."

Nate got out. The temperature was in the midsixties, and people were walking up and down the street in short sleeves. The trees next to the redbrick sidewalk were budding, and he could smell flowers on the breeze.

Tim took a big, audible breath. "Smell that? 'Behold, I will do a new thing. Now it shall spring forth—shall ye not know it?'"

"Isaiah 43:19," Nate murmured.

"Exactly." Tim nodded. "New life, new beginnings, new possibilities. Embrace it."

Nate gazed up at the big iron cross atop the stone church's spire. "What if she's not ready?"

Tim clapped a hand to Nate's shoulder. "If she's the one, then you wait. You pray for her, you prepare a safe place for her and you wait with eager anticipation for the day when she is."

Nate smiled his first genuine smile of the afternoon. Patience wasn't usually a problem for him, but when it came to Amanda, he had the feeling it might be easier said than done.

Cheryl was nothing like Amanda had expected. A good six inches shorter than Amanda with a warm, open smile and killer curly hair, she'd been nothing but helpful all day.

When Amanda's mom got delayed at the airport, Cheryl had even skipped dinner with Hayden to give Ivy a bath, read her a bedtime story and tuck her in. Ivy, who'd been delighted to hear that she was Hayden's grandma, had started calling her "Gammy Sherry" the moment they met.

Nate and his father-in-law stopped by to pick up Cheryl

after Ivy went to sleep. Cheryl took Tim out back to see the stars from the beach, giving Amanda and Nate a moment alone.

"How was Harvard?" Amanda asked.

"It was fine. How were things here? How's the wrist?"

"It hurts, but I've been icing it a lot. Cheryl was great. I didn't have to lift a finger all day."

"What time does your mom get in?"

Amanda glanced at the clock on her microwave. "She should be here in an hour or two."

"If you need anything tomorrow, just let me know."

"Thanks."

He looked at the darkened kitchen window and pushed a hand through his hair. "Did I scare you off the dance lessons for good?"

She laughed. That was *not* what she'd been expecting him to say. "Somebody's gotta make you look good out there."

"So…once you get your cast on, you're willing to give it another go?"

"Sure. Why not?"

He grinned, and…*oh, my.* That dimple. "Great. It's a date."

Her heart stuttered. A date?

A *date* date? Or a friend date?

She didn't have time to ask, though, because Cheryl and Tim came back in to say their goodbyes. Then the three of them drove away, leaving Amanda to reflect on the fact that, tonight, the idea of going on an honest-to-goodness date with Nate hadn't scared her or made her feel guilty at all.

Chapter Eleven

On Thursday night, Amanda couldn't get to the dance studio fast enough. Her mother was driving her up a wall.

The orthopedic surgeon had put her in a cast a few days ago, clearing her to go dancing this evening. She went an hour early, though, so she could talk to Ellen again.

The older woman rushed right over as soon as Amanda walked through the door. "I'm so sorry! I can't believe you broke your wrist! I should have told you not to take off your shoes after I waxed the floor!"

Amanda waved away her concerns. "It's okay, Ellen. With the cast, it really doesn't hurt at all."

Ellen wrung her hands. "I have liability insurance if you—"

Amanda shook her head. "Please don't worry about it. I have good medical insurance. It's covered."

"Are you sure?"

"Positive." She glanced around the studio, taking in the overall colorful vibe. She could envision exactly what she wanted to do here. She'd need to find a contractor who could execute her vision, but she was excited about it. "I actually came early because I wanted to talk to you again about buying you out..."

They adjourned to Ellen's office in the back and discussed

things again. In addition to finding a contractor, Amanda would need to find a real estate agent to put together an official offer.

When the bell over the front door jangled, they came back into the studio proper. Nate smiled at them. He looked freshly shaven, and he was dressed up more than he had been for their previous lessons: dark slacks and a light blue button-down shirt, cuffs undone and shirtsleeves rolled halfway to his elbows.

Her mind flashed to a memory of him playing the guitar at church on Sunday, where he'd been focused. Intense. Talented.

But selfless, too.

He wasn't using his musical skills to make a name for himself; he was using them to glorify God. Somehow, that made his talent even more appealing.

After greeting both of the ladies, he touched Amanda's cast and said, "You're a brave woman. You sure you want to try this again?"

"Absolutely. Last week was just a fluke."

A smile ghosted his lips. "Let's keep our shoes on this time, shall we?"

She inclined her head graciously, like the pageant girl she'd once been. "Let's."

Ellen turned on the music, instructing them to warm up by swaying. Nate put his right hand on her back, then gently held her right hand in his left. "Are you really feeling okay?"

"A hundred percent. Are *you*?"

"Honestly, it wasn't that bad. I wouldn't even have seen a doctor for it if you hadn't gotten hurt."

"Cheryl and Tim left for their bike trip?"

Nate shook his head in awe. "Those two are such go-getters. I hope I have that much stamina when I'm their age."

"Not too far off now, is it?" she teased. "A little birdie told me you're coming up on the big 4-0 pretty soon."

He grimaced. "Yup. That's me. Just about over-the-hill."

"Pssh. You're totally not."

Ellen paused the music and told them to try the basic box step—no traveling and no turns. Nate started leading, and Amanda could immediately tell that he'd gained confidence since the last time they'd danced. "Has somebody been practicing?"

He pursed his lips to quell his grin. "Somebody has."

"Wow." She felt a little breathless. It was nice not to be the teacher tonight, to let him take the lead. But then a sliver of jealousy worked its way into her head. "With who?"

He laughed. "Cheryl was all too happy to spend some time whipping me into shape."

Relief slid through her, followed by a healthy dose of sheepishness. She had no business feeling jealous—she didn't want to be more than friends.

Did she?

No. Her mother would have a field day if she thought Amanda was interested in Nate. She'd find excuses—flimsy, transparent, *embarrassing* excuses—to push them together the whole rest of the time she was here.

Plus… Miyoko. If Amanda ended up going to the medal ceremony for Pierce in Boston and saw his mother in person, she wanted to make sure her conscience was clear.

Ellen told them they could go ahead and work on their turns, so they started doing that. As Nate moved her around the dance floor, he said, "Can I ask you something?"

"Go ahead."

"You mentioned that Pierce was your best friend's older brother, right?"

"Mmm-hmm."

"How much older was he?" His shoulder tensed under her hand, and she tilted her face up, wondering why the question was causing him to worry.

"He was ten years older."

"Hmm." Still tense. "That's significant."

She gave a slight shrug. "I mean, it was and it wasn't. I was never a party girl, so I didn't feel like I was missing out on 'sowing my wild oats' or anything. And he was always really supportive of me. People hear about a thirty-year-old guy marrying a twenty-year-old girl and they assume he's either a controlling creep or an immature man-child. Pierce wasn't either of those things. He was confident in who he was, but he never tried to stifle me or put me in a box. He wanted me to figure out what would make me happy and go for it. He'd be thrilled if he knew I was going to use part of his life-insurance money to buy this place."

Nate stopped moving to the music. "Buying this place as in…here? The studio?"

Amanda grinned, excited. "I'm going to turn it into a women's exercise studio. With aerobics and kickboxing and a separate babysitting room upstairs. And maybe a little spa and a coffee shop or juice bar. I think that would be cool, especially in the summer, when all the tourists are here."

"Wow. That's quite a project."

"Obviously, it won't happen overnight. I still need to make an official offer, and then it'll probably be a couple of months before the sale closes. Then I'll need to find a contractor and do some renovations. So, at the earliest, we're probably looking at a grand opening next spring."

"Do you have training in how to run a business?"

"I took some business classes in college, and Cape Cod Community College actually has a whole certificate program for small-business owners! I'm going to take some of those classes this summer, and some of them in the fall."

"And you've already registered?"

She nodded, clocking the furrow on his brow. "Mmm-hmm."

"Wow." He blew out a quick breath. "So, you're here in Wychmere Bay for good, huh? Good for you."

"You sound skeptical."

"No, no." He held up his hands. "Not skeptical at all. I'm sure you can do anything you set your mind to."

"But?"

"But nothing." He forced a smile. "It sounds great. I hope it all goes smoothly for you."

"Thanks." Was he being genuine? It felt like he was holding something back, and it was taking the wind out of her sails. "Do you think it's a bad idea? Because I was thinking about how little time moms have to themselves, and how much easier it would be to get some exercise and practice self-care if you had a place where you could go and trust that your kids would be taken care of."

"I think it's a great idea. Childcare is a huge deal for young parents. I'm sure your gym would be really popular with new moms."

Okay, that sounded sincere. Good. She felt better. Doing this would require a big leap of faith, and if the people around her weren't on board with it, she wasn't sure she'd succeed.

"What are you going to do about the Candy Shack?" he asked.

That was the one part of this whole equation that had her a little apprehensive. "I'm not sure yet. I need to talk to Irene."

"Yeah," he said, taking her back into his arms for the waltz. "You should do that."

As they finished their lesson, Amanda couldn't help feeling as though something between them had shifted as a result of tonight's conversation, and not in a good way.

What she couldn't put her finger on, however, was why.

When Nate got home from the dance lesson, Hayden was doing his homework at the kitchen table. Seeing Nate, he sat back and grinned. "Dad and Ms. Kobayashi, sitting in a tree, d-a-n-c-i-n-g!"

Oh, the irony. Nate had been gearing up to ask Amanda out on a real date tonight—or at least tell her that he'd like to, when she was ready—but then she'd let him in on her plan to open a business here in Wychmere Bay, and he'd dropped it. Even if she was ready to move on and could get past the age gap, there was no way they should start something when she was settling in to life here and he was preparing to leave.

"How's the homework going, champ?"

Hayden shrugged. "It's fine. Got a math test tomorrow."

"What's eight times twelve?"

Hayden rolled his eyes. "I'm not eight, Dad. I know my times tables."

"So…eight times twelve is…?"

"Ninety-six."

"Good man."

"Did Ms. K bring Ivy to the dance class?"

Nate shook his head. "Remember? Ivy's grandma's in town to help babysit."

Hayden scrunched his nose. "You should tell them that I'll watch her if they want to go out shopping or something."

"I thought you had enough money for the chess trip after Grandpa Tim gave you that present."

"I do." Hayden took off his glasses and cleaned them on his shirt.

"But you're still looking for babysitting jobs?"

His son shrugged. "She's funny, Dad. And I haven't seen her for a while. And if I keep babysitting, I can save up for something else. Like books. Or college."

A week wasn't really *a while*, but it was cute that his son missed Ivy. Nate pulled out a chair and sat down. "Hey, I wanted to talk to you about something."

Hayden closed his math textbook. "What?"

"You know that Amanda and I aren't dating, right?"

Hayden frowned. "Yeah."

"So why did you make it sound like we were to Grandma and Grandpa Tim?"

"Oh, that." His son's shoulders sank. "Sorry. It was stupid."

"You made Grandma unhappy," Nate said gently.

"I don't get why she was so upset."

"When you love someone, seeing people moving on can feel like a betrayal."

Hayden picked at the dirt underneath one of his nails. "That's not fair, though. It's not like you're cheating on anyone."

Nate sat back, surprised. Since when did his son know all about cheating? "That's right, I'm not. Because I'm not dating."

"But even if you *were*, it still wouldn't be cheating, would it? You can't cheat on someone who's dead."

Nate sighed. "I wish you'd known her, champ. Then you'd probably understand why Grandma was upset."

"Other kids get stepmoms, even when their mothers are still alive—just divorced! Why do they get two moms and I get none?"

"Every family's different, Hayden."

"Do you feel like you're betraying Mom? Is that why you've never wanted to get married again?"

"No," Nate admitted, "not anymore. I'll always love your mother, but it's a nostalgic love now, not an active love."

Hayden pursed his lips in confusion. "What's the difference?"

"Well, I love you, so I do things for you, right? I have this house that I share with you, I buy food that we eat together, I help you with your homework and get you new clothes when you need them and spend time hanging out with you, yes?"

"Yeah…"

"When we love someone, we give of ourselves. We *want* to give of ourselves. And I can't do that for your mom anymore. She's not here to receive it. So I can think back on the memories and remember the good times and all the things I loved about her, and I can do my best to carry out the plans we made together, but that's it. It ends there."

Hayden crinkled his brow. "So it's kind of like that verse we were talking about a few weeks ago? 'Faith without works is dead'? Love without works is dead, too?"

Nate smiled. His son was a smart kid. "Kind of. Having feelings for someone is part of it, but backing up your words with selfless action is part of it, too. And receiving gifts of love from the other person in return? Well, that's a whole special kind of awesome."

"But you don't have feelings for Ms. K?"

Oh, man. Right back in the hot seat. "Well," he hedged, "I like her a lot, but she's a lot younger than me, so she might not share those same feelings."

"She likes you, though. I can tell. She laughs at your jokes, even the ones that are, like, super cringey."

"Excuse me?" Nate slapped a hand to his heart, miming offense. "My jokes are not cringey!"

"Ew, Dad. Don't be cheugy."

Nate bit back a smile. "Cheugy? That's a new one."

"It means you're trying too hard. Like, you just saying *cringey* is cringey."

"So you're saying I should *take the L*," he said, winking, "and stop talking?"

"Dad," Hayden groaned, clearly not wanting to hear him use any more Gen Z slang.

"All right, all right." Nate held up his hands. "I'm done."

"If you talk like that around Ms. K, she's going to think you're desperate."

Nate laughed. "I only talk this way around you, kiddo."

"And if you try to do that at church…" Hayden shuddered. "Don't. Just don't. None of the kids will take you seriously."

"I won't embarrass you at church. I promise."

"Good." Then Hayden paused, scrutinizing him. "Thirty-nine's not *that* old, is it? I mean, I know it's old, but you're not, like, ancient."

Nate pointed to the gray hair at his temples. "It's kind of old. Middle-aged."

"How old's Ms. K?"

"She's still in her twenties."

"Oh."

"Yeah. You see the problem, don't you? We're at different stages of life."

Hayden thought about that for a second. "But you're both parents, right?"

"Ye-e-s," Nate said slowly. "But her husband passed away much more recently than your mom. I don't think she's ready to have feelings for someone else just yet."

"Don't worry. You've got time to play the long game, Dad. She lives here now, just like us."

Nate didn't have the heart to burst his son's bubble by bringing up Boston.

Hayden would find out they were moving soon enough.

Chapter Twelve

May turned into June. Amanda found a real estate agent and made an offer on the dance studio. Ellen accepted the offer, and now they were just waiting for the escrow company to do what it needed to do before the sale closed.

Her mother wasn't excited about her plans to open an exercise studio, but Amanda chalked that up to the fact that her mother was still trying to convince her to move back to LA, so she didn't worry about it too much.

If all went well at her next appointment with the orthopedic surgeon, Amanda would be out of her cast soon, anyway, and her mother would be free to take her opinions about Amanda's life and life choices back to California with her.

In the meantime, she and Nate were still taking their Thursday-night dance classes, and he was getting better and better every week. The shimmer of possibility she'd felt the weekend after she'd broken her wrist had died down, but she was still looking forward to showing off their moves at the wedding, which was now right around the corner.

Planning a wedding shower with a broken wrist hadn't been a big deal, but decorating for the shower was another matter altogether. Fortunately, the Wise Widows were on the case.

Since Amanda was hosting the event at her house this afternoon, she'd sent Ivy and her mom out to the park for the morning. As soon as the door closed behind them, Sarah and Joan started hanging banners, arranging balloons and setting up photo-booth props in the backyard.

The theme for the shower, which was coed so that Bill, Nate and Hayden could join in the fun, was "Taco 'Bout Love." The balloons were a mix of smiling tacos, cacti and sombreros. There was a piñata full of candy rings, miniature chocolates and taco key chains, and Amanda had a few funny shower games up her sleeve, including one called "Cold Feet," where people would try to fish plastic rings out of a bucket of ice water with their toes.

Irene and Bill hadn't registered for wedding gifts, so Amanda had instructed everyone to bring gag gifts. She'd bought them an embroidered apron set declaring them "Mr. Right" and "Mrs. Always Right." Sarah, meanwhile, had found mugs proclaiming, "I love you" and "I know," and Joan had purchased custom bobblehead dolls that looked just like the happy couple.

"This is going to be hilarious," Amanda said, surveying the yard once everything was set up. The white hydrangeas in her flower beds were blooming, and the grass, which had been well-watered by a couple of recent storms, was a vibrant, sweet-smelling green. Best of all, though, was that it was warm and sunny, and the sun was sparkling off the nearby waves in pops of effervescent shine. "I can't wait to see their faces."

"You're a sweetheart for putting this all together," Sarah told her.

"I couldn't have done it without your help," she said, indicating both Sarah and Joan.

Joan gave her a grateful, watery smile. "Thank you for including me. You're a very forgiving person, and it means a lot."

Amanda looked away. She wasn't *that* forgiving. Just last

night she'd gotten upset with her mother for buying Ivy yet another party dress.

Her mom had insisted Ivy needed it for the wedding shower, but Amanda didn't like the way her mom spoiled her daughter with fancy clothes and kiddie makeup kits and dress-up dolls. If her mom insisted on buying Ivy new things, Amanda would prefer she purchase books and educational toys. The way things stood, it felt like her mom was priming Ivy for the pageant circuit. Although Amanda was grateful for her mother's help, she was also anxious for her to go back to California so she and Ivy could get back to their normal life.

And then there was the whole issue of the medal ceremony later this week. Her mom had been bugging her about that, too.

Her dad had already booked his ticket to Boston so he and her mom could attend, and her mom said it would look bad if Amanda wasn't there with them.

"I don't really care about appearances when it comes to this, Mom," Amanda had insisted the last time they'd argued.

"Well, did you care about Pierce? Because if you're not there, people are going to think you didn't."

On some level, Amanda knew her mother had a point, but still. She didn't want to go. Didn't want to meet the parents of the girls he'd saved from drowning and pretend like she was glad he'd done what he'd done.

And she didn't want to see or play nice with Caroline, either.

The bitterness she felt toward her former best friend continued to burn bright inside her, and she didn't know how to stop fanning the flames.

Nate's words from the night they'd done the tasting came back to her: *You feel what you feel. And whatever it is, it's okay.*

He was a good listener, and a good friend. Solid. Steady.

He wasn't angry with the doctors who'd misdiagnosed his wife and delayed her care. How had he done that? How had he let it go?

"I don't have all the answers, Amanda," he'd said, but from where she was sitting, it sure seemed like he had a lot more than she did.

God, she prayed, still feeling awkward and self-conscious in her newly rediscovered faith, *help me. I don't want to feel like this, but I can't turn it off.*

The guests started to arrive, and Amanda went into hostess mode. Bill and Irene were thrilled with the turnout, and everyone enjoyed the fish tacos the caterers grilled in the backyard.

Ivy squealed in delight when Hayden helped her bust open the piñata, and the two of them scrabbled to collect the vast majority of the loot that burst out onto the grass.

"Great party," Nate said, holding a paper plate that held a few remaining bites of a battered-cod taco.

Amanda directed a pointed look at his plate. "How many of those have you had?"

He laughed. "Too many. I've lost count."

"The lime sauce is good, isn't it?"

"So good."

"You need to save room for the cake."

His eyes lit up. "There's cake?"

"Vanilla with lemon-curd filling and buttercream frosting."

He tossed his plate into a nearby trash can, then rubbed his hands together in anticipation. "Sign me up."

"We're going to play some games first."

"Wedding showers are fun. How come the guys are never invited?"

She smirked. "You're here now, aren't you?"

"Hello, hello." Her mother floated over wearing a smart

silver sheath dress with a sheer chiffon wrap. "You must be Nate." She leaned in and kissed him on the cheek.

"Yes." He took a small step back. "And you are…?"

"Oh, you." She laughed. "Such a kidder. Can't you see the resemblance? I'm Marilyn, Amanda's mom, although I've been told we look like sisters."

Nate gave Amanda a surreptitious, blink-and-you'll-miss-it, wide-eyed look before smiling at her mother. "Pleasure to meet you."

"I've heard wonderful things," she gushed. "Except for the wrist, of course. That was unfortunate."

"I'm not the best dancer, but Amanda's been doing her best to whip me into shape for the wedding."

Marilyn leaned in conspiratorially. "She learned all her best moves from me."

Nate gave an uncomfortable laugh. "You taught her well."

Marilyn preened. "I taught her to sing, too. So much talent. And then she went and flushed it all down the toilet."

"Mom!" Amanda protested.

"Well, it's true, isn't it, princess? You don't sing anymore. Although I suppose in the end it didn't matter. You reeled in Pierce just fine without it."

Yikes. Her mother was in fine form this afternoon. Had she somehow managed to sneak alcohol into the event? She hadn't had a thing to drink since she'd arrived on Cape Cod, but once she started down that path, you could never really predict what would come out of her mouth…

"Did you try the tacos, Mom? They're so good."

Her mother pouted. "They're fried. Bad for the figure."

"Maybe have one with just the shredded cabbage and cheese?"

Ignoring her, her mother turned back to Nate. "Pierce was a good provider, a very good provider. He was smart like my husband—he planned ahead. But now my daughter's got all these cockamamie business ideas that are going to blow through what he left for her. She needs a man to sit her down and show her what's what."

Amanda wanted to hide her face in her hands. Her mother was embarrassing them both.

"Um…" Nate flashed Amanda a *help me* look. "I think her business plan is solid."

"Oh, pooh. You're just saying that because you're trying to impress her."

"Mom." Amanda took her elbow and attempted to steer her away from Nate. "Let's get you some water."

"Ninety percent of small businesses fail. And no one, not even her own godmother," her mom cried out, raising her voice loud enough to quiet the other guests, "will give it to her straight."

Irene marched over. "Marilyn. You're making a scene."

"Me? I'm only trying to help my daughter."

"Come inside."

"I'm just talking to my new friend Nate here," her mom said, grabbing his arm.

"Let's go in, Marilyn," he told her in a gentle voice, obviously trying to defuse the situation. "You can have a glass of water and relax a little."

"No, I'm waiting for someone."

A sense of dread washed over Amanda as Irene crossed her arms over her chest. "Who?"

"Oh, there she is." Her mother beamed and raised her hand in an enthusiastic wave.

Amanda wheeled around to see who'd arrived, disbelief turning her stomach to ice.

Caroline had stepped into her backyard.

And she was holding a baby.

Chapter Thirteen

Amanda gasped, her shocked gaze slamming into her mother. "What did you do?"

Her mom gave her an airy wave. "She's your best friend. It's time to bury the hatchet."

Amanda had never understood the term "seeing red," but it made sense now. She felt like the top of her head was going to shoot right off, her blood pressure rocketing it up to the sky.

"Whose baby is that?" she asked, voice shaking, as Ivy ran over to get a better look.

Marilyn laughed. "Don't be silly. Whose baby do you think it is?"

Amanda turned to Irene. "Get Ivy. I don't want her talking to Ivy."

Her godmother frowned. "She came all this way…and she's Pierce's family. Ivy's family. Her blood. Maybe you *should* go talk to her."

"No." Amanda shook her head. Couldn't they see what this was doing to her? Just the sight of Caroline was ripping her apart.

"Why don't you come inside for a minute?" Nate suggested, moving his hand to the small of her back. "I'll get you some lemonade and you can sit. Have a moment to think."

"I want her to leave, Nate." She felt wild-eyed. Panicky.

"I know you do," he said calmly. "Irene will ask her to leave. Just come inside with me."

She let him lead her into the house, where she sat in the living room, shaking all over.

He sat down across from her, leaning forward, elbows on his knees. "That's Caroline, isn't it?"

"Yes," she whispered, trying to slow her breathing and stop the shaking. But she was furious. So furious she might never speak with her mother again.

"You didn't know she had a baby?"

She wagged her head. "No."

"Where are your blankets? You're shivering."

"Hallway closet," she said, inclining her head in that direction. She was so angry she could hardly see straight.

He left and came back with a fuzzy brown blanket, which he draped over her lap. "Do you want me to make you some coffee or tea?"

"Could you just warm up a cup of water in the microwave?" She didn't have the energy to direct him to the caffeinated drinks just now.

He nodded and disappeared to do it, coming back a few minutes later and handing her a steaming mug. She took a sip and tried to calm herself down. He'd added honey and lemon to the water. The drink was soothing, and it helped.

"I guess I wrecked the shower, huh?"

He sat back and crossed his legs so that his left ankle was resting on his right knee. "I'd say your mom did a pretty good job of that all by herself."

Amanda winced. "She's not normally that bad."

"Is she an alcoholic?"

"No!" Knee-jerk reaction. "I don't know. She doesn't drink very often, but when she does, some of her more outdated opinions come out and stretch their legs."

"Does she drink around Ivy?" He looked serious and concerned.

"I haven't seen her drink anything this whole trip. Not until today."

Nate took off his glasses and rubbed the side of his face. "Why would she invite Caroline to Irene's bridal shower? Had Caroline even met Irene before?"

"Yes, but only through me. It's not like they're friends." And as for why her mother had invited Caroline, Amanda knew she was trying to force her to attend the medal ceremony.

"How do your parents know Irene, anyway?"

"She was my paternal grandmother's best friend. My grandma died right before I was born, and my dad thought asking Irene to be my godmother would be what she'd have wanted."

"I'm sorry your mom blindsided you like that."

"Thanks." She looked out the window. This room didn't face the backyard, but it did have a nice view of the beach. Was Caroline gone already? Had her outburst ended the party? And what on earth was she going to do with her mom?

"Do you want me to go out and check on things?"

"Would you?"

He rose from the couch. "Of course."

Amanda took a few more sips of her drink and worked on taking deep, calming breaths. This clinched it for her. There was no way she could go to the medal ceremony. If merely seeing Caroline could set her off like this, going to the ceremony would downright kill her.

Nate came back inside. "Okay, she's gone. Your mom's gone, too. Irene booked her a room at Sarah's B and B and she and my dad are driving her over, so you don't have to worry about seeing her again tonight."

Amanda let out a breath, her shoulders relaxing with the news. "What about everyone else?"

"Sarah and Joan are cleaning up. Everyone else went home."

"Where's Ivy?"

"She and Hayden are in the backyard trying to pull little rings out of a bowl of ice water with their feet."

Amanda put her hand to her face. "I'm the worst hostess in the world."

"That's not true."

"We didn't even cut the cake."

"Irene did it. She gave everyone a slice to take home."

Amanda chewed her lip. "I feel bad."

He shook his head. "Don't. Everyone had their fill of tacos. We all understand."

"I saw her and I just...panicked."

"It's okay," he said. "Everything's going to be fine."

She smoothed her hand over the brown blanket covering her lap. Because it was furry, petting it was calming, like petting a dog or a cat. "The medal ceremony for Pierce is this Friday. That's why she's here."

"I know. Brett invited me to go with him and Valerie."

"You're going?"

He nodded, and she sat with that for a second, unsure how it made her feel.

"My mom thinks I should go. That I'll regret it if I don't."

A corner of Nate's mouth twitched. "Your mom thinks a lot of things."

Some of the heaviness lifted, and a smile crept onto Amanda's face. "She *does*, doesn't she?"

"I thought you got your dance moves from cotillion. But turns out I was wrong. They're from her!"

Amanda did a facepalm. "Yup. My older sister taught me well."

"Older?" Nate teased. "I thought she was the younger sister."

Amanda laughed. "In her dreams." Then she got quiet again. "For real, though, it's embarrassing that she thinks I need a man to tell me how to spend the life-insurance money, and that she basically announced it to all the guests at the shower."

Nate hitched his shoulder. "The way she was acting, I doubt anyone put any stock in that."

Maybe, maybe not. Either way, she still felt insecure about it. "You don't think it's a bad idea? The exercise studio?"

"No, I told you before. I think it's a great idea."

She smirked. "And you're not just saying that to try to impress me?"

"Ha! I think we both know that ship's already sailed. I've done enough damage in the dance studio that you're never going to be impressed with me."

Did he really think she was that shallow? That, in her eyes, it was the dance moves that made the man? "That's not true. You have a lot of impressive qualities, Nate. If I was ever ready to fall in love again, I'd want it to be with somebody like you."

Nate went still at her words, and it took a moment for his mind to catch up.

If, she'd said, not *when*.

Like you, she'd said, not *you*.

He cleared his throat. "Thanks."

"I mean it." Her eyes were fixed on his. Clear. Bright. Honest.

Like sunshine after a storm.

It hurt to have to hold back how he felt about her. There was an actual ache in his chest from keeping the feelings dammed up inside.

But she wasn't ready, and he didn't have time to be patient. He was leaving for Boston so soon.

"Since your mom won't be here, do you need help with Ivy the rest of the day?"

Tucked beneath the fuzzy brown blanket, she looked fragile. Blond, beautiful and breakable. It made him want to bundle her up and protect her from anything that could do her harm. "I can probably manage."

"It's no trouble," he said. "Hayden'll be happy to spend time with her. He'll probably even cook dinner if you want."

"He's such a good kid."

"He really is. I can't believe he's going to be a teenager next year."

"Are you worried about it?"

"A little," he admitted. "Big kids, big problems, right?"

"He's got a good head on his shoulders. He'll be fine."

"I hope so. He and I talk about stuff, and we pray about it, but as a parent, there's only so much you can do."

"Before you had him, did you and your wife want more kids? Or were you only going to have one?"

A snick of sadness squeezed his heart. "We wanted more. A lot more. A whole houseful. Why? How about you?"

She gazed out the window, down to the beach. "We wanted more, too. Not a whole houseful, but at least two, maybe three."

Nate glanced outside, too. There was no wind today, and the water was calm.

"Pierce was kind of disappointed when we found out Ivy was a girl. He wanted a boy first. Of course, once she was born, he immediately changed his tune. She had him wrapped around her little finger from day one." She smiled wistfully.

"Was that a cultural thing, do you think? Wanting a boy?"

She shook her head. "That's the stereotype, right? That

Asian families prioritize boys over girls. I think that was more of a thing in China than it was in Japan, honestly, because of the one-child policy. But that wasn't it for him. It wasn't that he didn't want girls, he just wanted a boy *first*. He liked being a big brother, and he thought a big brother would look after his younger siblings."

Nate didn't want to upset her, but this was probably as good of an opening as he was going to get. "Caroline was just leaving when I went outside."

Amanda blanched. "Did you talk to her?"

"She's staying at the Sea Glass Inn tonight. She gave me her number in case you want to call."

Her mouth flattened into a stubborn line. "I don't."

"Are you sure?" She was so compassionate in most areas of her life that it was hard to watch her dig her heels in about this. He wanted her to have freedom—total freedom—from the anger and unforgiveness. But it was her choice to make. Her step to take. Not his.

Her expression wavered. "Is it a boy or a girl? The baby?"

"A boy, I think. He was wearing blue."

Amanda dropped her head, closing her eyes as though the news pained her. "How old is he?"

"Around one, probably. Maybe less."

A tear streaked down her face. "She was pregnant. The day he died. She was pregnant."

Nate stayed silent. It was clear that she was talking to herself.

"Did she know? Did she tell him?" She looked up at him as though he could give her the answers.

"I don't know," he said gently. "Do you want to go find out?"

Chapter Fourteen

"Haybee's doggie *loves* me!" Ivy squealed as the little dog licked her cheek.

"Don't let her lick your face, chickadee," Amanda said, grimacing as she turned to Nate. "The dog's had all her shots, right?"

"Clean as a whistle, I promise." He shot a glance at Hayden. "Can you hold her by the collar until she calms down?"

"Lucy," the boy instructed in a firm voice. "Down."

The dog backed off of Ivy and let Hayden pat her head, tail thumping.

"Are you sure you don't mind watching her, Bill?" Amanda asked Nate's dad.

The eldest Anderson stroked his mustache and shook his head. "Go do what you've gotta do, hon. Hayden and I have this covered."

She and Nate drove to the Sea Glass Inn in silence. She was nervous and not at all sure this was a good idea. What if she started panicking again? What if she just couldn't stand the sight of Caroline or the baby?

Ivy deserves to know her cousin. Do it for Ivy.

Nate glanced over. "You okay?"

She shook her head. "I'm freaking out a little."

He reached over and put his hand on her cast. "I've got you, shorty."

Despite herself, she grinned. "I think that's the first time in my life anyone has ever called me short."

He winked. "You're shorter than me."

"By what? Two inches? Three?"

"Three at least. Maybe four."

"Uh-huh," she said, deadpan.

"Seriously, though. I'll be with you every step of the way."

They turned onto Sand Street and she took a deep breath to tamp down her nerves. "Thank you."

Four circular tables with umbrella shades sat on the front lawn of the Sea Glass Inn, and Caroline sat at the one closest to the road, the baby in her lap, standing on her thighs and giggling.

Caroline stood when she heard the car doors slam, hefting the boy into her arms. Her hair was shorter than it had been before Pierce died, her smile more cautious. She hadn't lost all of her baby weight yet, but she looked nice in black pants and an aquamarine V-neck blouse with ruched sleeves.

Amanda had expected the anger to kick in again at the sight of her, but it didn't. Instead, a wave of nostalgia hit her. This woman had been her very best friend for years.

Amanda raised her hand as she approached. "Hey."

Caroline returned the gesture, then motioned to the table. "Do you want to sit?"

They sat. Amanda nodded at the baby. "What's his name?"

Caroline flipped him around so Amanda could see his pudgy little face. "Leon."

"He's cute."

"Thanks."

There were a few beats of awkward silence. *You're not freaking out, though. That's progress.*

Amanda glanced at Nate, and he gave her an encouraging smile. She was glad he was here. She wouldn't have done this without him. He took her hand in a show of support, and she let him.

"So…" she began, just as Caroline said, "I'm sorry. Your mom told me you knew I was coming to the shower."

Amanda slowly wagged her head. "No. I didn't know. About that, or about your baby."

Caroline had the decency to look contrite. "I tried to tell you. You blocked my number."

"How old is he?"

"Eleven and a half months."

"Your mom didn't tell me, either."

"Anytime she tried to hand me the phone, you hung up on her."

Amanda's face heated. *Daughter-in-law of the year right here.*

"I know you're angry with me," Caroline said, tearing up, "but please don't take it out on Pierce. Come to the ceremony. I won't even go if you don't want me to. Just go and be with my mom. Please. She needs it. The pomp. The circumstance. You and Ivy. And Nate, too, if you want him there with you."

Realizing her hand was still linked with Nate's, Amanda pulled it away. A big ball of guilt and anger and shame and sadness swelled up inside her. "Nate and I aren't together."

"Oh." Caroline's face creased in confusion. "I'm sorry. I thought—"

"Why didn't you go in the water that day, Caro? Why didn't you try to save him?"

The tears in Caroline's eyes spilled over, trailing down her cheeks. "I'm sorry. I wish I could go back and do it over again. He was my brother, Amanda, and I thought he could do anything. I loved him, I looked up to him my whole life. Even when they pulled that last little girl from the water,

even when we couldn't see him anymore, I never thought…
I just never thought…"

Amanda swallowed past the lump in her throat. She hadn't allowed herself to think the worst, either. For those three days he was missing, she'd still believed that he'd make it out alive, too.

"Did you know you were pregnant?"

Caroline sniffled. "Yes. I took the test the night before."

"Did Pierce know you were pregnant?"

Her sister-in-law nodded. "I told him on the ride up." They'd gone to Hampton Beach in New Hampshire that day, just the two of them. It had been a tradition of theirs to go on a brother-sister outing once a year on the anniversary of their father's death. Now, it was the anniversary of Pierce's death, too.

Amanda was afraid to ask the next question, because she knew her husband. Knew his values and his morals and his beliefs. And she knew that when Caroline answered the question, the anger she'd been feeding and petting and nurturing for the last year and a half would vanish and all she'd be left with was the heartbreak. The sorrow and the grief.

Leon, oblivious to the heaviness hanging over them, slammed his hand on the table once, twice, three times. Then he did it again, looking delighted at the noise.

He was mixed-race, like Ivy. Her baby girl's cousin. And they were only two years apart.

She blew out a breath. Nate was still sitting beside her. She could take strength in that, and in him. She could take strength in God, too.

He will my strength and portion be.

She could carry the weight of the sadness.

For her. For Ivy.

As long as life endures.

* * *

Nate could see the struggle playing out on Amanda's face. The sun was sinking lower in the sky, casting long shadows, but he was dialed in to every small shift of her expression, every hitch of her breath.

Help her, Lord. Help her to let it go.

She stopped struggling. She straightened. "Did Pierce… Did he tell you not to go in?"

Caroline started crying in earnest. "He said, 'Stay here. I've got this,' and I listened. I believed him. I wish I hadn't. Maybe it wouldn't have made any difference, but at least I'd know now that I'd tried."

Amanda reached across the table and touched one of her nephew's chubby feet. He giggled and cooed. "You were protecting your baby," she said, "and he was protecting you."

"He was a good brother," Caroline choked out, still crying.

"A good husband, too. A great one. The very best."

"I'm sorry," Caroline whispered, wiping at the tears on her face.

"Can I hold him?" Amanda asked, jiggling Leon's foot. Caroline handed him across the table and Amanda held him in front of her so that she could look straight into his face. "Hey, baby. Hey, Leon. I'm your auntie Amanda."

The little guy stretched out his hand and touched her cheek, then grabbed a lock of her hair.

She smiled as she gently disentangled his fingers from her hair. "Well, hello to you, too. It's nice to meet you, sir."

He bounced in her arms and babbled, "Ch-ch-ch!"

"Oh, you like choo-choo trains, do you? I like them, too. Choo-choo! Choo-choo!"

Leon squealed and kicked his feet. "Ch-ch-waa! Ba-da-ba-da-boo!"

Amanda shot a look at Caroline, who'd finally gotten her tears under control. "He's so verbal. Is he crawling yet?"

"Not yet, but he's been pulling himself up and standing in his crib."

"Good boy. You're raring to go, aren't you?" She flicked another glance at her sister-in-law. "How's Matthew?"

"He's good. He switched jobs last year. He's working at a digital marketing agency downtown."

"That's cool. Does he like it?"

"He does. There's more opportunity there, and he's learning a lot."

"Will he be at the ceremony?"

Caroline's dark eyes went wide with hope. "Will *you*?"

Amanda held up her cast. "I won't be able to drive myself just yet, but Nate's friend Brett is actually getting a medal at the ceremony, too, so I can probably hitch a ride."

Their gazes both flew to Nate, who nodded, humbled and grateful to have been present here with them this evening. Amanda might have dropped his hand at the first hint that there could be more than friendship between them, but that didn't matter. What mattered right now was the healing God was working in these two women's lives. "Absolutely. If there's no room in Brett's car, I'll drive you there myself."

Chapter Fifteen

Amanda brushed her big toe through the wave, skimming the shore. It was cool out now, a little before eight o'clock, and the sun was finally going down. The longest days here on Cape Cod were almost an hour longer than the longest days in LA.

She loved the extra daylight, although the humidity was something she could do without. She spread her arms and took a deep breath of the salty evening air. She was still wearing the sundress she'd worn for the shower, and it ruffled around her calves in the breeze. "After my cast comes off, we should go swimming."

"You'd want to go swimming after…?" Nate asked.

She felt lighter than she'd felt in a long time. Peaceful, more content. Finally, she understood what had happened that day, and it made sense. Pierce hadn't just gone in to save other people's children. He'd gone in for his sister and his nephew, too.

Amanda wasn't sure why that made such a big difference to her, but it did.

He'd gone in for his family. His blood.

"I was a lifeguard, you know. In college."

"I think you mentioned that to Joan that first night you both came to the Wise Widowhood meeting."

"Just one town over, at Lighthouse Beach." She tipped her face toward the wooden lifeguard tower a few yards behind them in the sand. "They have a tower just like that one. Two of the best summers of my life."

"Did you ever have to rescue anyone?"

"I blew my whistle a lot to tell boats and Jet Skis to move farther away from shore. Once or twice some kids got blown out past the buoys on their inflatables, and we went and towed them back in. Nothing serious."

"That's good," he said. "Cheryl wanted me to make sure you've got Ivy signed up for swimming lessons."

Amanda laughed. "Yeah, she brought that up with me, too, the day she was here."

Nate was carrying his shoes, but she'd left hers back near the dunes. A wave surprised her, swirling up around her ankles, and she jumped back, grabbing Nate's forearm for support.

"Watch out," he said. "Tide's coming in."

The light was fading, the sun painting the sky pink and purple and a bright, fiery orange as it fell deeper and deeper into the sea. Her hand was still on Nate's arm and she was grateful to him. So grateful. Today had been hard, but he'd stuck with her every step of the way. "Put your shoes down. Dance with me."

He let out an incredulous laugh, glancing over his shoulder to see if there were other people nearby. "Here? There's no music."

Grinning, she wrapped her arms around his neck, and he had no choice but to drop his shoes and move his hands to her waist. "But we've already taken off our shoes and everything."

"You and your barefoot dancing," he said, shaking his

head, but there was a smile on his lips and a twinkle in his eye.

Her breath caught in her throat. He was handsome, her Nate, and kind. So very kind.

She looked up at him as they swayed, the surf and the sea foam lapping at their toes. "You really helped me today."

"I'm glad I was there."

"No, like *really* helped me. I wouldn't have gone to see her if it hadn't been for you."

"That's what friends are for." He brushed a strand of hair out of her face, tucking it behind her ear, then put his hand back on her waist. It was warm. Steady. Comforting, but also surprisingly exhilarating.

Or maybe it wasn't so surprising. She'd been fighting her attraction to him from the moment they'd met, and she didn't want to fight it anymore.

What she felt for him—it went way beyond physical chemistry. And maybe it was still too soon to start something new, but in this moment, she simply didn't care. "What if I don't want to be friends?"

Confusion clouded his face, and he stopped swaying. "Amanda…"

She put her right hand on his cheek, stopping the words. He'd been freshly shaved earlier, but it had been hours since the bridal shower, and his skin was getting rough with five-o'clock scruff. Going up on her tiptoes, she felt his breath against her cheek. "I don't want to be just your friend."

"This isn't—"

"Shh," she murmured, moving a few millimeters closer as his breath hitched and his hands flexed on her waist. "I don't want to talk anymore. I want you to kiss me, Nate."

He made a sound in the back of his throat—a protest? A plea?—and then, finally, tenderly, his mouth met hers.

* * *

Her lips were soft, and the hem of her pretty, flowy dress was brushing against his shins in the wind. He pulled her closer, felt her nestle against him. She felt so good in his arms, but he shouldn't be kissing her like this. She'd had an emotional day. She was vulnerable, and he was taking advantage of that.

He broke away, and she let out a small sound of disappointment.

They stared at each other for a second. Her chest was rising and falling quickly, her breathing just as unsteady as his. She was still close enough that he could pull her back into the kiss with the barest hint of effort.

Lord, help me.

If he and Amanda were ever going to be more than friends, the timing had to be right. She couldn't be grieving, or reeling from a roller coaster of a day, or floating on a pink cloud of relief.

And he couldn't have one foot out the door on his way out of town.

"We can't do this," he said, scrubbing his hands through his hair so that he wouldn't reach out to hold her again.

Her forehead furrowed. "Why not?"

"Too much has happened today. It's clouding your judgment."

She rocked back slightly on her heels. "It's not."

"You can't tell me that what just happened with Caroline didn't affect you."

"Of course it affected me. In a good way, though. I feel like I finally have some closure, and maybe I can move forward now with my life." She took a step toward him, but he backed away.

"You're not thinking clearly."

She lowered her chin and rubbed her right hand against her cast. "I've liked you from the get-go, Nate, even when it makes me feel disloyal. Don't you like me?"

Her eyes were large and liquid, and her words were making him sweat. This felt like a test, a spiritual test, and he wasn't at all confident he was going to pass. "Of course I like you, but friendship is all I have to offer right now, Amanda," he said quietly. "You know that Hayden and I are moving to Boston soon."

"Not until the end of August. Can't we just…try this out? See where it goes?"

Another wave washed up around them, and as it fell back into the ocean, it sucked some of the sand out from beneath his feet. He wanted to explore this connection between them, but he had to put Hayden first. He had to. He'd promised Danielle he'd take care of their family, and going to Harvard and becoming a professor was the best way to do that. "I'm a pastor—I have to be intentional about everything. I'm not someone who can casually date."

"Haven't you given your notice?"

He hadn't—he was waiting until after the wedding, after he'd told Hayden. "This isn't about technicalities. It's about who I am. I'm not casual. I'll never be casual. If there's nowhere for this to go, I can't get involved. I won't."

"How do you know it won't go anywhere?" She was still watching him with those big blue eyes, but now the sheen in them had dimmed from hope to hurt.

"The PhD program at Harvard is a five-year commitment, and then who knows where I'll get a teaching job. You're putting down roots here. You bought a house. You're buying a business."

"That doesn't mean—" She took another small step toward him, and he held up his hand to get her to stop. If she touched him again, he might not be able to resist her, and if it was already this hard to walk away from her, how much worse would it be when he had to leave for Harvard?

"Please don't make this harder than it has to be. Of course I have feelings for you. But for this to work, we'd need time, and we don't have it." He took a breath, searching for something to say that would bring levity to a moment that had none. "Besides, I'm too old for you, anyway. You need someone who can keep up with you—in life and on the dance floor. And as that broken wrist proves," he said, nodding toward her cast, "that's definitely not me."

She didn't say anything for a good few seconds, and then, slowly, she gave a small nod, her lips an unhappy line across her face. "So I guess you agree with my mother after all, huh?"

He blinked. "Your mother?" He didn't agree with that woman on one single thing.

"That I need a man to sit me down and show me what's what not just with my finances, but with my relationships, too."

"That's not—"

Now she was the one who put up her hand, her chin quivering but her head held high. "Thanks, I guess, for giving it to me straight."

Chapter Sixteen

They drove back to Nate's house in silence. Inside, Amanda woke up Ivy, who'd fallen asleep in front of the TV. Then Bill drove the two of them home.

Wrung out, Amanda deposited Ivy on her bed without giving her a bath or brushing her teeth or even changing her into pajamas. After that, she went into her own room and promptly fell asleep.

Irene showed up early the next morning with two cups of coffee and a cup of hot chocolate for Ivy, who was—wonder of wonders—sleeping late.

"Where's my mother?" Amanda asked, sipping her drink.

"I told her to head up to Boston a few days early," Irene said briskly. "She left."

"She was drinking yesterday."

Irene nodded, her mouth pressed into a grim line.

"Where did she even get alcohol?" Amanda didn't have any in the house. "What am I going to do, Irene? This cast doesn't come off for eight more days. I can't have her around if she's drinking in front of Ivy."

"Bill and I will help you. And Nate, if you want."

Amanda closed her eyes in an attempt to shut out the humiliation. "Bill told you, didn't he? About what happened with me and Nate?"

"He only told me that, when you got back, you were upset. I assumed something happened with Caroline."

"No, it went well with her—"

"Praise the Lord."

"—but then I made a fool of myself in front of Nate."

"I'm sure you didn't."

The memory of it assailed her, humiliating her all over again. She'd known better than to put herself out there again, had made up her mind not to before she met him, but she'd felt so safe with him that she'd let her guard down. And then—poof.

He'd pulled the rug out from under her. And like a fool, she hadn't even seen it coming.

"I kissed him and he rejected me. He said I wasn't thinking clearly. That all he could offer me was friendship."

Irene slapped her hands on her hips. "Well, of all the idiotic—"

"I know," Amanda groaned, burying her face in her hands. She didn't need Irene to rub it in.

"Not you," her godmother said, her tone sharp. "Nate."

Amanda peeked through her fingers. "Come again?"

"You're the best thing that's happened to that boy in a long time. What kind of idiot excuse did he give?"

Amanda straightened in her seat. "He doesn't want to start something right before he moves."

Irene's face went slack. "He's moving?"

Oh, no—was it a secret? She knew that the church didn't know yet, and Hayden didn't know yet, but she'd assumed that Bill—if not Nate himself—would have told Irene. "He wants to be a professor, so he's getting a PhD from Harvard. But you can't tell anyone. He's not letting people know until after the wedding."

Color rose to Irene's cheeks. "Bill knows, doesn't he?"

Amanda nodded.

Her godmother narrowed her eyes. "Men and their secrets. But they're not the only ones, are they? What's all this about you starting your own business?"

Amanda bit her lip. This wasn't the way she'd hoped to present the idea to Irene. "Umm, surprise?"

Irene tapped her toe. "Come on now, don't keep me waiting. What is it? Where?"

"I made an offer on the dance studio. I want to turn it into a women's exercise studio with babysitting and a mini spa."

A grin lit her godmother's face. "Well, that's just perfect for you, isn't it? You can teach classes, have a little office upstairs, keep Ivy close by all day."

"That's what I thought, too. Only... I won't be able to do that and run the Candy Shack for you. I mean, it'll be a little while before the sale closes and I get all the construction done, so I won't desert you right away, but I know you wanted to retire and..." Amanda wrung her hands. She hated letting people down.

"Oh, pishposh. I don't want to retire. I only said that so you'd have a reason to move to Wychmere Bay."

"Wait...what? I thought you said you wanted to travel. With Bill. After the wedding."

Irene fluffed her perm. "Silly girl. I love that man, but traveling with him full-time? No, thank you. Our honeymoon will be plenty sufficient for us, believe you me."

"Oh."

"You'll still be able to cover the store while we're on our honeymoon, won't you?" Irene arched an eyebrow.

"Yes, of course. I'll be out of the cast by then and everything."

"Then it's settled. And no need to feel anything but excited about your new venture. You know I'll do whatever I can to help."

Amanda shook her head in wonder. "I can't believe you tricked me into moving here."

"Well, as your godmother, it's my honor and privilege to help guide you in life."

Glancing around her gorgeous kitchen—and out the window at her spectacular view of the ocean—Amanda couldn't help but be grateful for the guidance. She'd been lost when Irene had proposed she move here, and despite what had happened with Nate last night, she still had so much to look forward to here in Wychmere Bay. "I appreciate you."

Her godmother gave her a little wink. "Don't you worry, young lady. I know."

The drive to Boston for the Carnegie Medal ceremony was brutal. Actually, the whole week had been brutal. Nate couldn't get Amanda's kiss—or her crestfallen face—out of his head.

She hadn't shown up for the Wise Widowhood meeting on Tuesday night, nor had she come to their dance lesson last night, either. He wanted to talk to her, wanted to explain himself better than he had on the weekend, but he had the feeling that doing that would be like picking at a wound.

A clean break is better for her.

Ultimately, he knew, it would be better for him, too.

Except it wasn't clean. They lived in the same town. Hayden was still babysitting Ivy. And now, Nate was going to see her at this highly emotional event highlighting the sacrifice her heroic husband had made.

If it weren't for Brett, Nate might have skipped the ceremony, but he wanted to be there for his friend. It was a big deal, what Brett had done for Valerie and the twins, and Nate knew the younger man had a tendency to downplay his role in the daring rescue.

Not today, though.

Today, everyone at this event would honor his bravery, his selflessness, his steadfast courage, and they'd do the same thing for the other honoree, Amanda's late husband.

Pierce.

She'd loved Pierce without feeling disloyal. Loved him enough to move to his city, to bear his child, to marry him when she was fresh out of school.

Nate couldn't compete with that. He didn't want to.

Don't be ridiculous. Of course you do.

Danielle's face flashed through his mind. His chest throbbed, and he reached up to ease the ache. He would have loved her forever, but so much had happened since she'd passed away. He was a different man now, twelve years later, than he'd been back then. And the man he was now still loved her memory, but he also loved… Amanda.

Even if he couldn't be with her.

Even if he had to let her go.

Brett glanced away from the freeway for a second, clapping Nate on the shoulder. "You doing okay over there, man? You're awfully quiet." Valerie and the twins were in the back seat. The three of them were going to give a little speech at the event. Brett's sister, Chloe, and her husband, Steve, were driving up separately with their friends Laura and Jonathan.

"Yes, sorry. I'm fine."

"Surprised you didn't want to drive up to this thing with Amanda."

Nate reached up to adjust his glasses. "It was more a case of her not wanting to drive up with *me*."

Brett shot him a concerned look. "Really? What happened?"

The twins were playing "rock paper scissors" in the back with Valerie, too distracted by the game to pay any attention to the conversation he and Brett were having up here. "You probably heard about all the drama at the wedding shower last weekend, right?"

Brett flicked a glance at Valerie in the rearview mirror. She'd been there, and she'd likely filled him in. "Yeah," he confirmed, "I heard."

"Afterward, things between me and Amanda got…intense."

Brett raised an eyebrow but stayed silent, waiting for Nate to go on.

"She learned more about what happened the day her husband died, and me being there with her made her feel…closer to me, I guess. We kissed."

"Good for you." Brett's lips curved into a smile.

Nate shook his head. "It was a mistake. I shouldn't have done it. We're better off as friends."

Valerie snorted from the back seat. "Nate, please. Anyone within ten feet of you two can tell you're not just friends."

"She's not over what happened to her husband."

"And maybe she never will be," Valerie countered. "Can you honestly say you're over what happened to your wife?"

"It's been a lot longer for me."

"In Eating Disorders Anonymous, we have a saying: 'Sometimes quickly, sometimes slowly.'" Valerie had been anorexic as a teenager, but she'd come out stronger on the other side.

"Meaning…?"

"Meaning people change if they're willing to put in the work. But it happens in our own time. What may take months for one person only takes hours for someone else. And obviously, I don't know Amanda very well, but I know she's been going to your Wise Widowhood meetings. I know she's been going to church. I know you guys have been hanging out a lot, talking a lot. Do you think maybe, after what she learned last weekend, she's ready to take a step forward?"

He rubbed that tender spot on his chest again. "She said her feelings for me make her feel disloyal."

"Again, I'm no expert on widowhood," Valerie said, "but that sounds pretty normal to me."

Nate gave a slow nod. It *was* normal. He'd felt the same way himself for years and years.

Still did, if he was being honest with himself. Not about dating, but about deviating from the plans he'd made with Danielle.

He closed his eyes. He couldn't turn down a full ride to Harvard, could he? The plans he and Dani had made were for Hayden, above all else. Even if teaching college kids wasn't his dream, Nate could always go back to preaching once Hayden was done with school.

But he couldn't ask Amanda to wait for him for ten years.

"I'm moving to Boston at the end of the summer."

"You are?" Brett jerked his head toward Nate in surprise.

"I'm going to get a PhD in religious studies from Harvard." His words sounded rough even to his own ears.

"Well, that's... I don't know. We'll miss you, man."

Valerie gently placed her hand on his shoulder. "Is that what you want?"

Nate didn't know anymore.

But it's what he had to do.

Chapter Seventeen

The ceremony was being held in the courtyard of the Boston Public Library. Amanda had been here a few times during the years she'd lived in the suburbs, and she had to admit that it was a good choice for today. Impressive, yet peaceful. Quiet, but not too stern.

Inside, the library was all white marble and vaulted ceilings and imposing stone statues, but the lush green courtyard was centered around a serene fountain with a rectangular reflecting pool. One of the arcaded walkways was filled with white folding chairs for the event, and a podium was set up in front of the fountain. A couple of city officials in suits were milling around, greeting attendees.

Her parents waved at her, and she waved back. Her dad had flown in a few days early and stayed with her mom at one of the high-end hotels in Back Bay. Earlier, he'd confided in her that after they left Massachusetts, her mother had agreed to go to one of those high-end rehab programs, so Amanda was thankful for that.

Ivy tugged on her hand. "Gammy M!" she squealed, spotting Miyoko. Then she ran to her grandmother, who kneeled down and gathered the little girl in her arms.

Ivy hugged her back, then noticed Caroline and baby Leon. "Baby!" she shrieked.

Caroline laughed and let Ivy say hello, waving Amanda over as she did. Her husband, Matt, was standing next to her. "We saved you a seat," she said, indicating the place of honor right up front.

Amanda gave Caroline and her brother-in-law quick hugs, then turned to Miyoko. *"Konnichiwa."* She didn't know much Japanese, but Pierce had taught her a few phrases.

"So happy to see you," her mother-in-law replied in halting English. "I miss you."

Amanda teared up. "I missed you, too."

Caroline pulled an older man forward. "This is Ryu Shimada, my mom's fiancé."

Speechless for a second, Amanda's gaze flicked back to her mother-in-law, who was smiling at her fiancé with affection-filled eyes. "Nice to meet you," Amanda said, shaking off her surprise to shake his hand.

"Likewise," he replied, his speech as smooth as hers. His suit looked expensive, and his posture was stock-straight. He was dignified, and Amanda couldn't help but think that Pierce would have approved.

She also couldn't help but feel another chink of the armor she'd wrapped around her heart after Pierce died fall away. If her mother-in-law could find love again, why couldn't she?

Nate's face flashed through her mind, but she pushed it away. Her feelings for him didn't make her disloyal to Pierce, but they did make her feel stupid. She'd basically thrown herself at him and he'd pretty much told her she was out of her mind.

"Dr. Shimada is the one who bought Pierce's dental practice," Caroline explained. "That's how he and my mom met."

"Oh, wow. You're a dentist, too?"

"I am, and can I just say how very sorry I am for your loss."

"Thank you. Pierce would be happy to know that his practice is staying in the family."

"We haven't set a date yet," Ryu said, "but when we do, Miyoko wanted to ask if you'd let Ivy be a flower girl."

"Of course. She'll be there with bells on."

"And you will, too, I hope?" he asked.

She glanced at her mother-in-law and nodded. "Absolutely. I wouldn't miss it for the world."

Miyoko reached out and grabbed her hand, giving it a squeeze. "You visit me," she said. "Soon."

Amanda nodded. "I will."

They all sat as the two city officials situated themselves behind the podium. Ivy squirmed on Miyoko's lap, looking around at all the people gathered. "Haybee's dad!" she announced, hopping down and running toward him.

"Ivy!" Amanda grabbed at her daughter's wrist, but Ivy gave her the slip. Reluctantly, Amanda got up to retrieve her.

But Ivy wasn't interested in being retrieved. Nate had picked her up and she was chattering away. "Where Haybee? Where his doggie? My gammy M's here. It's a special day for my daddy."

"It is a special day," Nate said evenly, his eyes glued to Amanda's, "and I think your mom wants you to sit with her."

Why was her heart leaping around so hard at the sight of him? She'd known he was coming here with Brett. He hadn't caught her off guard.

It was the kiss. You can't shove that kind of fire back into a bottle.

She'd try, though. She had to try. It wasn't as though she could avoid him at the wedding next weekend.

"I sat with Mama in the car. We droved for eber and eber. It a special car! Mama sat with me in the back!"

"You must've had fun."

"Mama brought snacks! And books! And toys!"

"That sounds amazing."

Ivy looked around again. "Where Haybee?"

"He's at school today, sweetheart."

"But you camed for my daddy."

"And you." He tapped her nose. "And your mom. And my friend, Mr. Brett."

Ivy's little eyebrows squished together. "Who's Mr. Brett?"

Nate turned so he could point out Brett. "Your daddy saved some little girls from drowning, and Mr. Brett saved some little boys from a fire."

"But he didn't go to heaben?"

"Not yet."

"That's okay," Ivy said. "He go someday."

Nate gave Amanda a sad smile. "He will. God willing, we all will."

One of the officials tapped on the microphone, and Nate set Ivy on the ground. She ran back to Miyoko, who wrapped her arms around her and rocked her back and forth.

Nate, meanwhile, stuck his hands in his pockets. "How're you doing with all this?" he asked, nodding at her in-laws.

"Fine. Better than I expected, actually."

"Good."

Their eyes locked, and it was awkward, but there was nothing Amanda could do about it. She wasn't going to be the first one to look away.

"Well…" He shuffled his feet. "We should probably sit."

"Probably."

"I admire him, you know. Pierce. 'Greater love hath no man than this, that a man lay down his life for his friends.'"

"What verse is that?"

"John 15:13."

She nodded. It was a nice sentiment, although, like everything today, it was bittersweet.

Nate took a small step forward, intensity burning in his eyes. "Amanda, I wish—"

"If you'd kindly take your seats, folks," the official who'd tapped on the mic now said into it. "We're about to begin."

The ceremony was moving, and Valerie and the twins ended it on a high note with their sweet speech about Brett. Nate had it on good authority that Brett was planning to propose this weekend at his restaurant's grand reopening, and he hoped Valerie would say yes.

After he got home, he took off his jacket and tie, then sat in the family room working on his Rubik's Cube. It was mindless, which was just what he wanted. He wasn't sure how long he sat there before his dad came into the room and plopped into his armchair.

"You're home late."

Nate looked up. It was way past Hayden's bedtime, so he hadn't even bothered going upstairs to say good-night. "Steve and Chloe wanted to treat everyone who was there for Brett to a steak dinner up in Boston."

His dad stroked his mustache. "Nice of them. Was it good?"

"Delicious." In truth, Nate hadn't had much of an appetite since the night of the wedding shower. Turning Amanda away had tied his stomach in knots.

"How'd Amanda do with everything?"

"She wasn't at dinner, obviously, but she seemed to hold up well during the ceremony. Dabbed at her eyes a few times when the parents of those girls were speaking, but she accepted the medal without breaking down. She's strong."

His dad was silent, but the silence didn't feel companionable—it felt loaded.

Nate set down the Rubik's Cube on the coffee table. "What?"

"You put in your notice yet at church?"

Nate shook his head. "After the wedding, Dad."

"Are you sure? Couldn't you see about deferring going to Harvard for a year?"

"Why would I defer?"

"Amanda told Irene what happened on the beach last weekend."

Nate took off his glasses and rubbed his eyes. He shouldn't ask, but at the same time, he wanted to know. "What did she say?"

"You kissed her?"

"I did." The words sounded leaden. Nate *felt* leaden. He'd always thought of himself as a stand-up guy, and he didn't like it that he'd led Amanda on.

Before he'd found out she was buying the dance studio, he'd thought maybe, if things went well between them before he moved, they could date long-distance for a few months and then he'd ask her to marry him and move to Boston. But if she owned a business here, there was no way she could move up there—let alone wherever he went once he was a bona fide professor.

"You like her," his father said.

"We're at different places in our lives, Dad. We have different goals."

"Do you really?" His father leaned forward and snatched the Rubik's Cube off the coffee table, twisting it this way and that until he'd made a checkerboard pattern. "Do you actually *want* to be a professor? I'd never heard you mention it until you told me you got in to Harvard."

"I want Hayden to have the best start in life. I don't want him to be saddled with big student loans."

"How do you know he'll even want to go to college?"

Nate scoffed, taking the Rubik's Cube from his dad and changing the checkerboard pattern into flowers. "Mr. Chess Champion? Of course he'll want to go to college."

"He could join the military or go to trade school or, I don't know…invent some crazy computer app and move to Silicon Valley for all you know."

Nate pursed his lips. "Unlikely."

"You took out student loans, you know."

"Yes, Dad," he said dryly, "I recall."

"They didn't sink you. Why do you think they'd sink Hayden?"

Nate raked a hand through his hair in frustration. His dad didn't get it. He just didn't get it. "This is my son we're talking about. I'd do anything for him. I only want the best for him."

"And *I* only want the best for *you*."

"It's not the same."

"It *is* the same."

"No," Nate insisted, his voice rising, "it's not."

"Why not?"

Nate sprang to his feet. He was losing his temper, and he never lost his temper. "Stop pushing this."

His father rose as well. "No. You're being bullheaded. Answer the question."

Nate clenched his fists. "What question?"

"Why is me wanting the best for you different from you wanting the best for Hayden?"

"Because you already gave me the best, Dad! A stable home, a two-parent family. As a kid, I didn't want for anything. I had two parents who loved me, but because I didn't fight harder for Dani in the hospital, Hayden only has me!"

"Nate." His father looked dismayed.

Nate didn't feel so hot himself. He thought he'd turned this all over to God a long time ago, but apparently he hadn't. Not really.

Or, if he had, he'd taken it all back.

He collapsed into his seat and stuck his head in his hands.

"It wasn't your—" his father began.

"Don't."

They sat in silence for a few minutes. Nate just wanted his dad to leave. What kind of pastor was he? Who was he to stand up in front of his church on Sundays and preach to them about freedom and faith and forgiveness, when he didn't even have his own house in order?

He was a hypocrite—the worst kind of hypocrite. He'd been deceiving himself about his spiritual well-being this whole time.

"Maybe it's a good thing I'm about to resign. I'm not fit to lead a congregation."

"What? No."

"I didn't think I still felt guilty about it, Dad. I thought I was free. And here I've been talking to other widows and widowers week after week, telling them that God wants them to have hope for the future when I'm still clinging to the past and beating myself up for things I'll never be able to change."

"Grief's not linear, son. You know that."

"I know, but—" Nate scrubbed his hands over his face "—I feel like such a fraud."

"You're not a fraud. You're a man who's had some setbacks in life but who's doing his best every day to serve God and serve others. That's nothing to be ashamed of."

"I wish I'd pressed those doctors more."

"You don't have a medical degree. You didn't know."

"I want to do right by Hayden. She'd want me to do right by Hayden."

"You are doing right by Hayden. Every day, just by being his dad, you do right by Hayden. Go back to school if you want to go back to school, but don't do it because you're trying to prove something to someone who's dead and buried. Dani knew you loved her, she knew you'd love your boy. That's all she'd want from you, Nate. Love. That's all."

His father got up and squeezed his shoulder, and then he went upstairs to bed. Nate sat in the darkened living room for a long time, praying for clarity about love and loss and human frailty.

In the end, all he knew for certain was that life was a gift from God.

The question now was: How did he want to live it?

Chapter Eighteen

Amanda had managed to avoid Nate since the medal ceremony in Boston, but it hadn't been easy. He'd called, but she hadn't answered. He'd texted, but she'd left his messages unread.

He'd come to the Candy Shack a few times, too, and Amanda had found excuses to hide in the back room of the store.

She knew that hiding was borderline ridiculous, but really, how much rejection was a woman supposed to take?

She got it, not wanting to start a relationship right before moving. It was disappointing, but it made sense. What had really stung was him telling her that her judgment was bad, and that she wasn't thinking clearly. That she was acting like a child.

She'd heard that enough from all five of her brothers—and, of course, from her mother—when she was growing up.

Pierce had been the first man to truly believe in her. He'd trusted that, even though he was older than her, she knew her own mind.

She'd thought Nate had that same kind of trust in her, as well, even if all they could ever be to one another was friends. But nope. He'd made that clear that night on the beach. It didn't matter how sweet or patient he was with Ivy. If he didn't believe in her, she didn't want him in her life.

She'd need supportive people around her while she was building her business. People who would build her up instead of tearing her down.

But now it was almost time for the rehearsal dinner, and she couldn't avoid Nate all night. The reception tomorrow would be at Brett's restaurant, Half Shell, but the rehearsal dinner tonight was going to be a catered clambake in a tent on the front lawn of the Sea Glass Inn. Irene had been talking about it all week: raw bar, lobsters, clam chowder, red potatoes, corn on the cob, watermelon—the whole nine yards.

First, though, Amanda had to get through the rehearsal itself, which Nate was presiding over, since he was going to be the officiant at the wedding.

Sighing, she did the wrist-flexor stretch Steve Weston had shown her at her physical therapy appointment earlier this week. Her cast had come off and she was grateful to have full use of both her hands, although her left one was still quite weak.

Ivy bounced in her chair at the kitchen table, where she'd been coloring. "Mama, I drawed a picture for Haybee!"

Amanda bent down to examine it. "Let me see, chicka-dee."

On the page, there was a pink stick figure and a blue stick figure holding hands under a smiling yellow sun. "Honey, that's adorable. He'll love it."

"Haybee is my friend. My bestest, bestest friend."

"You're fortunate, aren't you, that you have a nice friend like Hayden."

"His doggie loves me, too!"

"I know! She gave you lots of ooey, gooey, slobbery doggie kisses!" Amanda leaned down and pressed a few quick kisses of her own to her daughter's cheeks. Ivy howled with laughter.

"His daddy's my friend, also! He droved all the way to see me on the special day for my daddy in heaben!"

Amanda gave her daughter an indulgent nod. She wasn't going to confuse her by explaining that Nate would have been at the ceremony anyway, for Brett. "He's going to be at the rehearsal tonight, telling you where to walk and stand for the wedding."

"I get to throw fowlers!"

"Yes," Amanda said. "Flower petals. Tomorrow, when you're walking down the aisle. Not today."

"I get to sit next to Haybee!"

"And you have to be a good girl. No talking or wiggling."

"I be quieter than a moose!"

"A moose?" Amanda chuckled. "I think you mean a mouse."

"No, Mama, no-o-o-o-o." Ivy leaped off her chair and ran into the family room, digging through her toy box until she found what she was looking for and victoriously held a little stuffed moose up high in the air. "Morton the quiet moose!"

"Aww, look at Morton. He's so sweet." Amanda gave his furry head a little pat. "Do you want to bring him to the rehearsal? He can remind you not to be noisy."

"Okay. I go put on his sweater." She took the moose up to her room, where she kept the clothes for her doll collection. Amanda smiled wistfully as she watched her go.

Ivy was going to be so sad when Nate and Hayden moved to Boston.

Amanda, though? She'd only be relieved.

Nate had been trying to talk to Amanda all night. He'd been hopeful when she and Ivy had entered the church for the wedding rehearsal, but although Ivy had run straight over to Hayden, Amanda had hung back, waiting until Nate started walking everyone through what would happen during the ceremony to even glance his way.

Afterward, she and Ivy slipped out before he and Hayden had finished turning off the lights and locking the door to the church. And now, at the rehearsal dinner, she was still eluding him, gliding away every time he started moving in her direction.

The temperature tonight was pleasant—even with the wind picking up and the sky clouding over—and the guests at the clambake were dressed nicely. Not cocktail attire, but not casual, either. The women were wearing sundresses or dressy slacks with cardigan sweaters, while most of the men were sporting khaki pants, golf shirts and blazers.

It was a large gathering—almost as big as the wedding reception would be. Out-of-towners, like his in-laws and Amanda's parents, were here, along with half of Wychmere Bay.

The white tent where the tables and buffet were set up had its sides rolled up, letting the sea air billow through. Hayden had his plate heaped high with lobster, potatoes and corn on the cob. He had on one of those plastic lobster bibs, too.

"Got enough food there, champ?"

"Nope." His son grinned, depositing his plate at one of the sit-wherever-you'd-like tables. "I'm going back up for the chowder and the watermelon."

Nate shook his head. Kid had a hollow leg. Nate had no doubt he'd be scouring the dessert table soon enough, snagging plenty of the sweets on display—key-lime-pie squares, cannoli cupcakes and sand-dollar sugar cookies.

Irene sidled up next to him. She was beaming tonight, her red lipstick getting a good workout.

"Feeling good?" Nate asked. "We're not going to have

to drag you to church tomorrow kicking and screaming, are we?"

She served him a nice big helping of side-eye. "When you find a good one, young man, you hold on tight. You don't run away screaming."

"My dad's a fortunate guy."

"Your father knew a good thing when he saw it. Some of his family members—" she paused and gave him a pointed glance "—are a little slower on the uptake."

Chuckling, Nate slapped a hand to his heart. "Ouch."

"You made a big mess of things with my goddaughter."

"I know, and I'm trying to make it right, but she won't talk to me." He watched Amanda crack open a lobster claw and use a crab fork to dig out the meat for Ivy. He could march over there right now and say his piece, but he didn't want to make a scene, and he definitely didn't want to put her on the spot in front of Ivy.

"Happily for you," Irene said, "the ceremony isn't the only thing we're rehearsing tonight." Nate shot her a quizzical look and she dipped her chin toward the portable dance floor the caterers were laying down as they spoke.

"Seriously? I thought you were saving the bulk of the festivities for tomorrow."

She winked at him. "When you get to our age, you stop putting off 'til tomorrow what you can do today."

"I doubt she'll want to dance with me."

"Who's the bride in this situation? It's my big day, my big moment. What I say goes."

"It's not your day yet, Irene."

She waved her hand dismissively. "Close enough."

"I don't want to make her uncomfortable."

"You *already* made her uncomfortable. Now, it's time to

fix it before the awkwardness between you two ruins my wedding."

Nate snorted. "Tell me how you really feel."

"I think you leaving your ministry is a mistake."

He took a breath. "So do I."

Irene blinked. "You do?"

"Yes." His dad had been right. Nate wasn't interested in becoming a professor. He already had a job he loved right here.

Irene took him by the shoulders and gave him a little push. "Then what are you waiting for, young man? Get over there and ask my goddaughter to dance."

If there was one thing Amanda knew for sure, it was that Irene and Bill knew how to throw a party. The lobster was delicious, and the Wise Widows she was sitting with were making her laugh. If the rehearsal dinner was this much fun, she could only imagine how awesome the wedding was going to be.

Provided she didn't have to interact too much with Nate.

Of course, as soon as Ivy had a few bites of food in her, she ran off to sit with Hayden, who was at a table with Cheryl and Tim. The wind blew through in a gust, blowing napkins to the ground, and the caterers rushed to roll down the sides of the tent, buffering everyone from the wind. As the tent flaps went down, the background music got louder, and the twinkle lights strung up all around the tent lit up, making some of the ladies at Amanda's table gasp in delight.

Nate tapped her on the shoulder. "Excuse me. May I have this dance?"

Amanda twisted in her chair to look up at him. Still so handsome. Those blue eyes. That dark hair. It wasn't fair that she was still so attracted to him after the way he'd shut her down, but she supposed that was life. After what she'd gone through with Pierce, she was certain she could handle whatever it threw at her. "Oh, I don't think there's dancing tonight."

"But there is," Sarah informed her. "And look! Bill and Irene have already gotten it started."

Sure enough, Bill and Irene were twirling away on a dance floor that had been set up toward the back of the tent.

"Whoa," Amanda said. "They're good."

"Want to go give them a run for their money?" Nate asked.

"No, thank you."

"Go!" Joan and Sarah both prompted her. "Live a little."

Sighing, she stood and followed Nate to the dance floor. She didn't want to be rude.

"With shoes or without?" he asked.

She smirked. "I think you can handle keeping your shoes on."

"How's your wrist?"

She rotated it in a small circle. "It's weak, but it's nice to have the cast off."

"I can imagine." He drew her onto the dance floor and placed one hand lightly on the back of her left shoulder, while holding her right hand loosely in his left. The music that was playing wasn't waltz music, so they ended up doing a weird half waltz, half sway hybrid. "I've been trying to get a hold of you all week."

She shrugged. "Sorry, not sorry."

"Okay," he said, holding up his arm so she could do a little twirl, "I deserved that."

His even-keeled manner was annoying her, and she decided to ruffle his feathers. "You kissed me like you meant it, Nate, and then you told me my judgment was bad and I wasn't thinking clearly."

"I know. That was stupid. I was worried you were going to regret the kiss, but I shouldn't have phrased it like that."

"I might be younger than you, but I'm not a child."

"I know you're not."

"I know my own mind."

"I know you do. You're stronger than any woman I've ever met."

She might not be succeeding in ruffling his feathers, but she was definitely feeling confused. "You can't say things like that to me."

He drew her closer, his hand warm and sturdy on her back. "Why not?"

"Friends don't talk to each other like that."

"I thought you didn't want to be friends."

"I don't!" Boy, he was really making this difficult. Maybe she should walk away right now, but she was curious to hear what he was going to say next.

"Well, good." He squeezed her hand. "I don't, either."

"Excuse me?"

"I don't want to be your friend. I want—no, I *need*—to kiss you again."

"But..." Her eyebrows drew together. "What about everything you said about not being casual?"

"I'm not casual. I'll *never* be casual when it comes to you."

A thrill raced through her whole body, even as her mind urged her not to get too far ahead of herself—this man had let her down before. "Wh-what does that mean?"

He dropped her hand and moved his fingers to her cheek, stroking lightly. "It means—"

"Hayden!" someone shouted. "Wait!" Both Amanda and Nate spun toward the sound, only to see Hayden running out of the tent toward the beach, Ivy hot on his heels.

Tim was on his feet, his face creased in a frown. Nate

moved quickly in Tim's direction, but Amanda took off after the kids. Ivy couldn't be trusted alone near the water, and Hayden had looked too upset to keep an eye on his little friend.

Outside, Ivy was only a few yards away, screaming, "Haybee! Haybee!" The wind had picked up a lot since they'd arrived, and it was whipping Ivy's hair around her head like she was in a blender.

Amanda grabbed her, getting down on her knees so she could see her face-to-face. "What happened, honey?"

"Haybee so sad he crying!"

Crying? That boy was usually as calm and steady as his father. What on earth was going on?

She watched him sprint down the beach toward the jetty, where white-capped waves were crashing against the rocks, and a sick feeling uncoiled inside her chest.

Not the jetty, Hayden. Not there.

A couple of other people had poked their heads outside, and Amanda caught sight of Sarah and Joan.

"Go back inside the tent with Ms. Sarah," she ordered, giving Ivy a little push in that direction. "Find Grandma and Grandpa or Miss Irene."

Then she kicked off her heels, picked up her skirt and ran.

Chapter Nineteen

Hayden was fast, and he'd had a head start, so he was way ahead of Amanda. "Hayden!" she cried out, but her voice was lost to the wind. Her hair kept getting in her face, too, and she didn't have a hair tie to pull it back into a ponytail, so she had to use one of her hands to hold it out of her eyes.

She pushed forward, the sand gritty under her feet, as the waves crashed high on the shore, depositing clumps of seaweed, driftwood and other ocean debris in her path.

He wouldn't go out on the jetty, would he? It was too dangerous right now; the waves were too high.

But he was headed straight for it, so she pushed herself to run harder, run faster, even as the wind made it hard to breathe.

"Hayden!" she yelled again, as he took the first few steps onto the rocks. She was still too far away, though, and he couldn't hear her. He didn't even turn his head.

The sun was setting behind the clouds that had blown in, turning the steely sky even grayer. Some of those rocks jutted up at almost ninety-degree angles. He'd turn back when he got that far, wouldn't he? Surely, he wouldn't try to make it to the tiny lighthouse at the end.

He was a kid, though, just a kid. And kids didn't always

have a lot of common sense. Even kids who seemed mature, like Hayden.

She hit the edge of the jetty, the place where the rocks met the sand. "Hayden!" she screamed one more time, hoping he'd hear her, hoping he'd stop.

He didn't. He was walking out farther and farther, at the point now where the spray from the waves must be soaking his pants.

She glanced over her shoulder, hoping that Nate or one of the other guests was right behind her, but there was no one. She was alone.

Ivy's face flashed through her mind, then Pierce's.

He'd died trying to save someone else's kids. She'd been so mad at him for that—and mad at God and Caroline, too.

Yet here she was, thinking about attempting the very same thing.

The last vestiges of her anger fell away. She understood. She finally understood—down to her bones—why Pierce had done what he'd done.

At the same time, though, fear crowded in. *God, please. It's too dangerous. Make him turn around. If anything happens to me, Ivy will be an orphan.*

But Hayden didn't stop or turn. He kept walking out farther.

Those rocks would be slippery tonight, covered in algae, and the waves were only getting stronger. Before too long, it would probably start to rain.

The same icy panic she'd felt when Ivy had gone missing washed over her. This was Hayden, Nate's Hayden—and he was in real danger. But her daughter needed her. She couldn't put herself in harm's way, too. *What do I do, Lord? Please tell me. What am I supposed to do?*

And then, a sense of calm descended on her. A sense of peace and calm.

You do the right thing. It was like Pierce was right there with her, holding her hand, speaking straight to her heart. *Put one foot in front of the other and do the next right thing.*

Taking a deep breath, she stepped onto the first boulder that made up the jetty. It was on the sand, so it was still dry. Before long, the rocks got wet, but she kept walking, keeping Hayden in her sight.

The path was slick, and there were spiky dried barnacles that pricked her feet with almost every step. She hadn't yet been hit by a wave, but she was drenched in sea spray, and she could see the waves breaking over the rocks up ahead.

Turn around, Hayden, she willed him, but he kept going, headed for the lighthouse, where the end of the jetty met the sea. She kept going, too, stepping over deep puddles and crevices between the rocks. She almost slipped a couple of times, but she threw her arms out for balance and managed to stay upright.

When she got to the boulder that jutted up at a ninety-degree angle, she got down on her hands and knees and crawled around it. Just as she found her footing again, she gasped as she got hit by a wave that knocked her sideways, and she decided she might be more stable if she stayed down low, moving forward on her hands and her feet.

Her newly healed wrist ached as she crawled forward, and she felt the barnacles slash at her palms and her toes. Looking ahead, she could see that Hayden had made it to the lighthouse, where the water exploded around him like fireworks every time a wave hit the rocks.

Stay there, kiddo. I'm coming.

Another wave struck, soaking her, and she shivered, then crawled forward again. She was pretty sure her hands and feet were bleeding, but she pushed forward despite the pain, clinging to the rocks with her fingertips where she needed to.

When she got within walking distance of the lighthouse, she called out, "Hayden!"

The boy looked over in surprise from where he was sitting with his back against the small stone structure. "Ms. K!"

He made as though to stand, and she shouted, "Don't move! Stay right there!"

Fortunately, he obeyed, even as another wave slapped against the rocks and smacked him in the face.

She reached the lighthouse and threw herself against it, grateful to have something solid at her back.

"Ms. K, what are you doing here?"

"It's too dangerous to be out here right now, Hayden. I was scared you were going to fall in."

He hugged his knees to his chest, his teeth chattering. "I'm okay."

"You're freezing."

"So are you. Your lips are blue."

She pressed a hand to her face. "Are they?"

"Like Ivy's were the night I found her out here."

Amanda shuddered. Both of her hands were bleeding, although not seriously. They were just surface wounds. "You know how dangerous it is out here during a storm. What were you thinking?"

He frowned and looked out to sea. "I don't know. I wasn't thinking, I guess. I just wanted to get away from everyone."

"Why?"

"We're moving and my dad didn't even tell me. I had to hear it from Grandpa Tim."

"Your grandfather told you about the move tonight?"

"At the dinner table. He was talking to somebody about it, how my dad was going to be a Harvard man just like him. And he starts classes in August. Some of my friends are gone for the summer, so I won't even get to see them before we leave! It's not fair. He should've asked me if I wanted to go. 'Cuz I don't. But even if we have to, my dad should've told me before school let out. At least then I could've said goodbye."

"Oh, honey, that's tough. I'm sorry you found out like that."

"Grandpa and Irene are here, my chess team's here, you and Ivy are here… I just don't get it. What's so special about stupid Boston?"

"Your dad wants to do something different with his career."

"Why? He's always telling me how important it is to help people. He helps people *now*. He doesn't have to become some stupid professor to do it."

"Maybe he likes helping young people like you. The world needs good teachers."

"It needs good pastors, too. Besides, I thought…" His cheeks went red, and he looked away.

"What?" she prompted.

"I thought he liked *you*."

Another wave splashed them, and Amanda sputtered a little, tasting salt water on her lips. She pushed her sea-soaked hair out of her face. "He does like me, honey. Your dad and I are good friends."

"Yeah, but I thought…" His chin wobbled. "I thought maybe you were more than friends. I thought maybe I was finally gonna get a mom. I thought maybe Ivy was going to be my little sister."

He looked so miserable that Amanda reached over and put her arm around his shoulders, pulling him into a half hug. She might not be clear about what was going on with her and Nate, but she was perfectly clear about this. "Listen, I may not be your mom, but I'll always be your friend. You saved Ivy, and that makes you part of my family, whether you live here or in Boston or in Timbuktu, okay? So you can be Ivy's honorary older brother regardless of what does or doesn't happen between me and your dad. We're blessed to have you in our lives, because you're a great kid. But right now," she said, looking up at the ominously dark clouds in the sky, "we need to get back to shore. Because once it starts raining, it's going to get even worse out here, and I don't want you to get hurt."

He took off his glasses and wiped his eyes with his wet sleeves. "Okay."

"Boston's a fun city. You'll like it there. And it's not very far, so I'm sure your dad will let you come back to visit all the time."

"I hope so."

Amanda held on to the lighthouse and got to her feet. Then she held out her hand to Hayden and helped him up, too. "You go first, honey. It's slippery, so watch your feet."

"I didn't know it would get so scary out here."

"I know you didn't. It's okay. Just go slow." She could see that a few people from the rehearsal party had collected along the shore, and one man—Nate—was halfway out to them along the rocks. Amanda waved, hoping to show him that they were okay.

As she lifted her arm, though, another huge wave broke against the boulder they were standing on. Although she was able to brace herself against the lighthouse to stay up-right, Hayden was a few steps ahead of her, beyond the light-house's reach, and she watched in horror as the swell of water knocked him off balance...and propelled him head-long into the sea.

Chapter Twenty

Nate's heart seized in terror.

No.

The wave swept Hayden off his feet and into the dark surge of the ocean, and Nate was too far away to reach him.

Just like when Dani was dying in the hospital, he was too far away.

Not my son, Lord. Please. Not my son.

The riptide near the jetty would grab him—if it hadn't already—and smash him against the rocks.

No, no, no.

Amanda was right there, but she wouldn't try to save him, and Nate couldn't even blame her. He still remembered what she'd said to him when she'd told him that Pierce had drowned saving those three little girls: *I'd never put the life of someone else's child ahead of Ivy's.*

But then, astonishingly, in the blink of an eye, she did.

She leaped in, and his heart seized all over again, because now he could lose both of them. Right now. In the ocean. He could lose them both.

Keeping his eye on the exact spot they'd gone in, he forced his feet forward. It was slippery on the rocks, but it would be faster to get to them on foot than trying to swim against the current.

There was a choking noise, and he realized it was him, struggling to breathe against the vise that was squeezing his chest.

Please, God. Please, God. Please.

He'd do anything—*anything*—if they'd just be okay.

If Hayden died because he'd been angry with Nate over a misunderstanding… If Amanda died before he could tell her that she was so much more to him than just a friend…

It would break him. He knew it. It would shatter his whole heart.

"Nate!"

He heard someone calling out to him, but he refused to slow down, refused to take his eye off the place where Hayden had fallen and Amanda had jumped in, not even to glance over his shoulder to acknowledge whoever was following him, trying to help.

He was a good swimmer. It was too dark to make out anything that was happening in the water from here, but if he could just reach that spot, he'd go in and find them. He didn't care how long it took him. He'd find them. He'd pull them out.

"Nate!"

He stilled.

That voice—*her* voice.

It wasn't coming from behind him.

He whipped out his phone, turned on the flashlight. Shone it out across the water and…there. There!

Two heads bobbing in the water.

Oh, thank You, God. Thank You.

They were sixty or seventy feet away from him on the harbor side of the jetty, which meant the waves were calmer and much less intense.

Were they okay? He was still too far away; he couldn't tell. And was one of them—he squinted—*towing* the other?

Hayden could be hurt, or not breathing. No way was he just going to stand here and wait to find out. He shone the flashlight into the water right below him to check for submerged rocks, dropped his phone and jumped.

The seawater was bracing, and he had to do a hard front crawl—keeping his head above water the whole time so he wouldn't lose sight of Amanda and Hayden—to get away from the jetty's pull.

"Are you okay?" he shouted as he swam. Swimming in the dark, fully clothed, was definitely a challenge, but he'd get to them if it was the last thing he did.

"We're good!" Amanda yelled back, and he kept swimming. *Talk to me, Hayden. Talk to me.*

It had started to rain, but it wasn't a deluge, just a drizzle, and he could see now that four arms were slicing in and out of the water, moving both Amanda and his son nearer to shore. Relief poured through him, powering him on.

"Dad!" Hayden laughed as Nate got closer. "What are you doing?"

"You fell in!"

"Doesn't mean you had to jump in, too!"

Nate slicked some water out of his face and treaded water. "You're okay? You're both okay?"

"Hayden got the wind knocked out of him when he fell, but he's fine now, right, honey?"

"I lost my glasses."

"It doesn't matter," Nate said. "Come on. Let's get you onto dry land."

After a few minutes, Nate's feet touched sand and he grabbed his son and crushed him to his chest. "Don't you ever—*ever*—do that again."

"I'm sorry, Dad. I didn't mean for that to happen."

"And you," Nate said, turning to Amanda as his eyes filled with tears of gratitude. "You saved him. You saved my son."

"He's a good swimmer," she replied, deflecting his praise. "He would have been fine."

"Marry me." The words were out before he'd had a chance to think them through, but he wouldn't have stopped them even if he could have. He loved her, and he'd never drag his feet about telling her that ever again.

She and Hayden both gasped. "What? No. You don't mean that. It's the relief talking."

"I *do* mean it. Marry me," he said again.

"Nate." She laughed incredulously. "What about Harvard?"

"I'm not going to Harvard. That's what I've been trying to tell you all week. I declined my spot in the program. Hayden and I are staying here."

Her mouth fell open as Hayden's brow furrowed. "But Grandpa Tim said—"

"Grandpa Tim's information is outdated. I was going tell him I'd changed my mind after the wedding, champ. I'm sorry you heard about it the way you did."

"We're not leaving?" Hayden seemed almost afraid to believe it.

"Nope."

"Dad!" Hayden hugged him tighter. "That's the best news I've heard all night!"

The group of people standing on shore had gotten bigger, and Brett, Steve Weston and Jonathan Masters were wading out to them. "Everybody all right?" Brett called out.

"We're fine," Nate called back, marveling at the fact that it was true. Hayden was fine, and Amanda was fine, too. He wasn't losing either one of them tonight.

The three younger men helped them out of the water. There were blankets onshore, and they all wrapped up tight.

Nate was surprised to find that his legs were shaking. "Aftermath of the adrenaline rush," Brett told him. "It'll pass."

The paramedics arrived and evaluated Hayden. They confirmed that he was right as rain—just cold and wet.

As they trudged back to the Sea Glass Inn, Nate kept his arm wrapped around his son's shoulders. Amanda, likewise, was walking with Ivy plastered to one of her legs. He could tell that he'd shocked her with his proposal. Maybe it was too soon, but he'd let the dust settle, and then he'd ask her again.

After all, there was no rush. Now that he was staying in Wychmere Bay, they had all the time in the world.

The next day, as Amanda was getting ready for the wedding, the doorbell rang. She was in her bridesmaid dress, but her hair was still down and her makeup was only half-on. It was hard to get ready when your hands were as cut up as hers were from chasing Hayden onto the jetty last night.

She went to the door, anyway, thinking her parents might have swung by.

But it wasn't her parents, it was Nate, looking dapper in a dark gray suit and a light purple tie that matched her dress. Her heart beat wildly. He hadn't meant what he'd said last night, had he?

And if he had…what in the world would she say?

There was no denying that she had feelings for him, and she was thrilled he was staying in Wychmere Bay, but… marriage? After only two months?

She wasn't about to jump into marrying anyone this fast. She had to be sure that the man she was pledging her life to would be a good father to Ivy, and—whether Nate was a pastor or not—she couldn't be certain of that just yet.

In all likelihood, he'd been joking—carried away by the

intense emotions of last night. Or, if he hadn't been joking, she prayed that he'd understand why she couldn't say yes.

At least not right now.

He held out a bouquet of a dozen two-toned roses—the blooms a mix of cream and pink. "For you."

She took them and inhaled the delicate scent. "They're gorgeous. Thank you."

"Can I come in?"

She held the door open for him.

When he walked into the family room, Ivy looked up from her stuffed animals. "Haybee's dad! You camed to meet my animals! This is Morton," she said, petting her little brown moose. "And this one's Slider and Baldo and Dally Dalamo," she added, pointing to her penguin, eagle and armadillo.

"Hello, Morton and Slider and Baldo and Dally Dalamo," Nate said. "Very nice to meet you."

Ivy scooped up all four of the stuffies and hugged them tight to her chest. "They want to go to the beach! Haybee's dad, you take us there!"

Endearingly, Nate looked sorry to disappoint her. "Sorry, sweetheart, not today. Today we're going to the wedding."

"Oh, yeah! I going to dance and dance!"

Amanda smiled. "That's right, chickadee. But for now, why don't you take your stuffies to your room and lie down with them? If you want to have energy to dance, you're going to need a little nap."

"Okay, but Baldo not tired. He want to stay here with you, Haybee's dad." She handed the little eagle to Nate, whose lips quirked up.

"Baldo," he said, as Ivy left the room. "Cute."

"I suggested Baldy, but we were reading the *Where's Waldo?* books, and she settled on Baldo."

He laughed, and the sound was deep and rich. "I remember those books. Have you introduced her to the *I Spy* series yet?"

She shook her head.

"We might still have some lying around. I'll ask Hayden to take a look tomorrow, see what he can find."

"That'd be great." She set down her flowers on the coffee table, feeling fidgety. She didn't know where to begin.

"So, about last night—" he started.

"How's Hayden?" she interrupted.

"He's good. Needs new glasses, but other than that, he's fine. Psyched for the wedding this afternoon."

"And you're—" she tilted her head to the side "—really not going to Harvard?"

He smiled. "No."

"Because of me?" she asked, holding her breath. It was too much, him giving up an opportunity like that for her.

"No," he said. "Not for you. For me. Dani was the one who always wanted me to be a professor. I like being a pastor. I don't want to spend the next five years training for a job I don't really want to do."

The relief made her knees wobbly. "Okay, good. Because we've only known each other for a couple of months."

"Did my proposal last night scare you?"

"A little," she admitted. "But I know you didn't mean it."

"Amanda, I did mean it. I'm not going to ask you again right now, because I know you're not ready, but I love you and I want a relationship with you. I had some things I needed to work out for myself, but I'm sorry if I ever made you feel like I questioned your judgment or maturity. Like I said last night, you're the strongest woman I know. And as you proved out on that jetty, you're the bravest one, too. Hayden said he was panicking and didn't know which way was up, but you pulled him to the surface. After everything you went through with Pierce, you dove in for my son. For that, I can never repay you, but if you'll let me, I'll spend the rest of my life trying."

She still felt scared, but there was also a rush of warmth—a stream of hopefulness—pooling inside her that was impossible to ignore. "You don't need to repay me, Nate. Since the night we met, you've been there for me in ways no one's ever been there for me before. You don't owe me a thing."

"I thought I was happy before I met you, but I was so scared of letting down another person I loved that I'd closed myself off. Last night, when I thought I was going to lose you *and* Hayden, it almost broke me, but you…" He stopped, fighting to control his emotions. "But God…"

She reached up to touch his face. "And you…love me?" She needed to be sure she hadn't hallucinated that part.

His smile lit up his whole face. "I've loved you from the very beginning, from the first time you kicked off your shoes and stepped on my feet."

Chuckling, she stepped forward in her stockings and stood on his toes. "Like this?"

"Just like that." His hands—careful and steady—went to her waist. His voice was a rough whisper across her lips.

She tilted her face up, and he kissed her. It was gentle. A promise of many more to come.

"Don't be scared of me, sunshine," he murmured. "Your happiness is all I want."

"Is that my new nickname? Sunshine?"

"It's what your smile feels like to me. Sunshine. But we can always use something else, if you'd prefer. Like shorty!" His eyes twinkled with mischief. "You seemed to like that one, too."

She shook her head, amused. "Start calling me shorty and I'll smack you. Sunshine's good."

He kissed her again until she put a hand to his chest and stopped him. "We can take this slow, right? Because I think there are a few things I need to work out for myself, too," she said, thinking about the exercise studio. Pierce had left her a lot of money, but she wanted to know she could stand on her own two feet, just in case.

"We can take it whatever speed you want. And slow might be better for the kids, anyway."

Thinking back to the conversation she'd had with Hayden last night on the jetty, her lips curved into a smile. *Maybe, but then again, maybe not.*

"It felt like Pierce was there with me last night, on the jetty." She'd always been open with Nate about her feelings for Pierce, and she wasn't going to change that now.

"Then I owe his memory a debt of gratitude, too."

"I get it now, why he did it. It wasn't about Caroline or her baby. It was just the right thing to do."

Nate moved his hands from her waist so he could wrap her in his embrace. "Doesn't make it easier, though, does it?"

She shook her head. Her heart had been broken when she'd met him, but now, it was finally starting to mend.

In Japan, there was an art form called *Kintsugi*, where broken pottery was repaired with precious metals like silver and gold. The damage wasn't hidden; it was highlighted. But in highlighting it, it was also transformed into something rare and beautiful. Something that could be both old and new.

That's how she felt about her heart these days. There would always be cracks, there would always be weaknesses, but Nate loved her in spite of them—maybe even *because* of them.

Like sunshine after a storm, God was giving her another chance to love and be loved, and she'd take it. Gladly. She was latching on to that gift with two hands and holding on tight.

Nate inched back from their embrace and tipped up her face so he could see her eyes. "I know you had a life before me. I know you loved him deeply, and I'm glad you did. I'm absolutely fine with taking things as slow as you need, but I just—" He stopped and took a deep breath. "Do you think one day you could love me, too?"

It hurt her heart that he even had to ask. "I don't have to think about it, Nate," she said, reaching up to touch his cheek. "I already do."

Epilogue

Okay, so there was slow, and then there was *glacial*. Now that she and Nate had been dating for a full year, Amanda was beginning to regret that the words *take it slow* had ever crossed her lips.

After Nate's impromptu proposal the night before Bill and Irene's wedding, she honestly hadn't expected that the second one would take quite this long. She'd held her breath on Christmas, then on New Year's, and then again on Valentine's Day. She'd held her breath on Nate's fortieth birthday, on her twenty-seventh birthday, and after the grand opening of her exercise studio, too.

Things there were going well. As she'd taken her business classes at Cape Cod Community College, the scope of the studio had changed. In addition to offering women's exercise classes, the studio—which she'd named Mom & Me Movement Studios—also offered classes that moms could attend *with* their kids, including music and movement, art and science, and a bubbles and drones class that sold out week after week.

The kiddie classes were quite popular, as was the babysitting room. Amanda taught a couple of classes, took a couple of classes with Ivy and generally enjoyed the flexible working schedule she'd been able to create.

It was great for being able to spend time with Nate and Hayden, especially since Nate's schedule meant he usually only had Sunday afternoons and Mondays off.

She and Ivy had joined the little choir that sang at the nursing home on Saturday mornings, and Ivy *loved* going to the children's room during Sunday services. She also loved it when the four of them—Amanda, Ivy, Hayden and Nate—spent Sunday afternoons together doing beachfront scavenger hunts, playing checkers, flying kites, walking Lucy or baking something sweet and then decorating whatever came out of the oven.

Today, they were making chocolate-glazed doughnut cookies, and Ivy was having a blast decorating them with sprinkles, gummy bears, peanut-butter chips, crushed Oreos and Froot Loops.

Nate was right next to her, encouraging her to mix all the toppings together and pile them high. Hayden, meanwhile, had a more refined palate and was mostly decorating his cookies with one topping at a time: mini marshmallows on one, shredded coconut on another.

"Have a bite, Mama!" Ivy waved a cookie at her.

"No thanks, chickadee. I'm getting a sugar high just looking at it."

Ivy turned to Nate. "Have a bite, Nate-Nate." She'd stopped calling him "Haybee's dad" a few months ago, opting for Nate-Nate instead. Amanda thought it was adorable, Hayden thought it was hilarious and Nate just rolled with it, throwing silly nicknames right back at her—much to Ivy's delight.

"Don't mind if I do, Ivy-Lou." He took a big chomp. "Mmm. Delicious! Those green-apple gummy bears really bring out the flavor of the Oreos and peanut-butter chips."

Ivy giggled and took her own bite while Amanda and Hayden traded grossed-out looks.

"You guys want to stay for dinner tonight?" Amanda asked. It's what they usually did on Sundays—she'd make a big pot of pasta or the boys would go get takeout from one of the restaurants on Main Street and bring it back to her house. Then they'd watch a movie or play a card game together. Uno, War, Go Fish and Rook were games they all enjoyed. Hayden was also in the process of trying to teach Ivy how to play chess.

Nate and Hayden exchanged a quick look. "I'm going over to my friend Tyson's house tonight," Hayden said, "but there's something I wanted to ask you first."

Amanda leaned forward. "Of course, honey. What is it?"

Hayden pushed up his glasses. "Actually, maybe my dad should go first."

She turned to Nate, who cleared his throat. "I asked Irene and my dad to watch Ivy tonight so you and I can go out."

"Oh, nice. Where are we going?"

"I signed us up to learn some Latin dances at a community dance event in Hyannis."

Amanda clapped her hands. "Fun!" Over the last year, they'd continued their Thursday-night dance lessons, perfecting the waltz and trying a little tango, foxtrot and quickstep, too.

"You up for some salsa, rumba and maybe a little cha cha cha?"

"With you? Always." She grinned.

"I made dinner reservations for us, too. You said you wanted to try Ocean's Edge, right?"

"Nate!" That was one of the nicest restaurants on Cape Cod, second only to Brett's Half Shell, of course. "What's the occasion?"

"Do I need a special occasion to take my girl out for a night on the town?"

"I guess not, but—"

"I'm kidding. Actually, I was hoping you might want to celebrate something with me."

He dropped to one knee on the kitchen floor. Her heart pounded as happiness flooded her whole body.

It's finally happening. Finally!

He reached out and took her hand. His Adam's apple bobbed as he swallowed. "Amanda. Sunshine. When you saved Hayden the night of the rehearsal dinner last year, I didn't think I could ever love you more, but every day, you prove me wrong. Every day, what I feel for you gets bigger and bigger, better and better, brighter and brighter. This year has been a dream, and I don't ever want to wake from it. Will you marry me?"

He held out a beautiful gold engagement ring with a yellow stone in the center, a halo of small diamonds surrounding it.

Joy swelled inside her chest and she nodded rapidly, blinking back tears. *Yes, yes, yes, yes, yes.*

"Yes?" Nate whispered.

"Yes," she echoed quietly, then laughed and found her voice. "Yes!"

Hayden cheered, and Ivy cheered, too. Nate slid the ring onto her finger, then kissed her hand before getting to his feet and pressing a chaste kiss to her lips. "I love you."

Amanda stared at the radiant cut gemstone in her new engagement ring. It was gorgeous, but she was worried he'd spent way too much. "This isn't a yellow diamond, is it?"

"It's golden beryl, also known as the sunshine stone."

She fanned her face. He was so thoughtful. She was going to start crying all over again.

"Do you like it?" he asked.

"I love it," she admitted, "but I love you more."

He kissed her again, then lifted her off her feet and spun her around in a little twirl.

"Mama!" Ivy exclaimed, pulling on her sleeve. "Is Nate-Nate going to be my new daddy?"

Amanda kneeled down in front of her daughter. "You'll always have your daddy in heaven, but if you want, Nate can be your daddy, too."

Ivy squealed with delight. "Haybee! I get to share your daddy!"

"Pretty cool, isn't it?" Hayden said. Then he turned to Amanda. "That's actually what I wanted to ask you. Now that you're marrying my dad, will you adopt me and be my mom?"

Now she was crying for real. "Nothing would make me happier, Hayden. I can't wait to be your mom."

He leaned down and tweaked one of Ivy's pigtails. "How about you, silly? Do you want to be my sister?"

She squealed again and hugged his leg. "I be the bestest sister eber!"

"Yeah, you will be." He held out his hand for a fist bump, and Ivy enthusiastically complied.

After a couple of group hugs and a bunch more of Ivy's excited squealing, Amanda and Nate dropped Hayden off at his friend's house, then took Ivy over to Bill and Irene's. They were, of course, thrilled to hear the news, and immediately offered to stay over at Amanda's house with Ivy and Hayden for the honeymoon.

Over shared plates of lobster tagliatelle pasta and filet mignon at dinner, she and Nate agreed that they wanted to take the kids on the honeymoon with them. They also agreed that—since this was a second wedding for both of them—they didn't want gifts, fanfare or a big to-do.

In fact, the more Amanda thought about it, the more she

wanted something small and simple. She almost suggested that they just take a trip to the courthouse on Main Street, but she knew that Nate would—understandably—want a religious ceremony rather than a secular one. And to be honest, she wanted that, too.

That's how, a month later, a small group of their loved ones gathered in her backyard for their outdoor wedding, which Nate's father-in-law, Tim, was officiating. Amanda was wearing a long, yellow sundress and holding a bouquet of sunflowers, blue hydrangeas and little white daisies. Ivy, who was also wearing a yellow polka-dot dress, had a matching bouquet.

Nate and Hayden were standing in front of the white wedding arch sporting light gray suits with pale blue ties that matched the color of the hydrangeas. Amanda had asked both her father and her mother-in-law to walk her and Ivy down the aisle.

Miyoko had cried last night when Amanda showed her the pendant necklace Nate had commissioned a jeweler to make out of her engagement ring to Pierce. It was simple and beautiful—an acknowledgment that Pierce would forever be a part of her and Ivy's lives.

"How blessed are we," Nate had said after he gave it to her, suggesting that she use it as her "something old" for the wedding ceremony, "that God's given each of us two great loves in our lifetimes?"

And as Amanda walked down the aisle as the birds sang and the sun shone and the waves crashed on the beach beyond her backyard, that's exactly how she felt: Healed. Happy. Blessed.

* * * * *

Dear Reader,

I started writing this book just a few months after I lost my last living grandparent, and having a front-row seat as Nate and Amanda navigated their grief journeys helped me work through some of my own sorrow.

Finding love in our fallen world can be a challenge, and finding it for a second time after a great loss can be doubly daunting. I hope that Nate and Amanda's story gave you hope that healing is possible and happiness is attainable, even when it comes hand in hand with grief.

Would you like to see what life is like for Amanda, Nate, Hayden and Ivy five years after the wedding? Will Nate and Amanda have a baby together? Will Hayden have to take out big student loans to go to college?

Visit MeghannWhistler.com/newsletter and sign up for my mailing list, and I'll send you a special bonus scene where you can see them living out their happily-ever-after ending in everyday life!

I'm always thrilled to hear that someone enjoyed one of my stories. Please feel free to email me at Meghann@ MeghannWhistler.com anytime!

Wishing you love and light,
Meghann

HARLEQUIN
Reader Service

Enjoyed your book?

Try the perfect subscription for Romance readers and get more great books like this delivered right to your door.

See why over 10+ million readers have tried Harlequin Reader Service.

Start with a Free Welcome Collection with free books and a gift—valued over $20.

Choose any series in print or ebook. See website for details and order today:

TryReaderService.com/subscriptions